Other Books by MEINDERT DeJONG

Far Out the Long Canal

Far Out

the Long Canal

by
Meindert DeJong

Pictures by Nancy Grossman

HARPER & ROW, Publishers
New York, Evanston, and London

FAR OUT THE LONG CANAL

For **BEATRICE**

Contents

Far Out the Long Canal

1

Winters Ago

MOONTA couldn't skate. In school he was the only one in the big room of the fourth, fifth, and sixth graders who couldn't skate. In the whole school everybody could skate except maybe the tiniest kids in the first couple of grades in the little room. But he—Moonta—was nine years old going on ten, and in the fourth grade. What made it worse, he was big for his age.

All the other kids in the big room had learned to skate before they'd started school. Moonta's father always said that in this northernmost village in the northernmost province of the Netherlands that was the right order of things—skate before you walk. That was a joke, of course, but a proud joke, with almost a little bit of truth in it.

Of course, Moonta couldn't help it that he couldn't skate. It was now four whole winters since there'd been ice on the canal. Four winters ago there had been a week of ice, but during that whole week of ice he had been sick. Everybody else, the whole village, his mother and father—everybody— had been skating on the canal, but he'd had to stay in bed. Long before Mother would let him out of bed, the ice had gone, and since then there had only been wet, foggy, miserable, sad winters.

Aunt Cora had come to take care of him that last week of ice four winters ago. She couldn't skate anyway—the only big person in the village that couldn't—so it was only proper that she should come. It left Mother free to skate with Father down all the canals of the whole province, to all its eleven towns. That wasn't unfair. Mother and Father were the village champions.

What was unfair was that he really hadn't been sick that last week of ice four winters ago. Why, all he'd had was a cold. Of course he really had been sick the winter before— sick with pneumonia. Oh, he'd been sick! And Mother was deathly afraid of pneumonia. That was because her only brother, when he was young, had died of pneumonia. He'd had a cold, but he'd gone skating, and he'd gone through the thin ice. But even with his cold he'd only gone home long enough to change his clothes, and then he'd gone out skating again. Then he'd got pneumonia, and then he'd died. So it was no wonder, really, that Mother had kept him in the house with a cold that last week of ice four winters ago.

What Mother couldn't have known was that the week of ice, when he'd been five years old and ready to learn to skate, would be the last ice. So it certainly wasn't his fault he couldn't skate. You couldn't learn to ice skate on fog or water, or over cobblestone streets.

Well, at least now it was winter again. But still there was no snow, no ice, no skating—nothing but fog and misery and wetness. It was the deadest winter yet, not even a flake of snow so far. And next winter he'd be ten years old and in the fifth grade and still not able to skate. As big as he was for his age, he'd be almost a big person then, like Aunt Cora. He'd be as big and shameful as Aunt Cora. The whole family was ashamed of her.

Moonta sat glooming on the gloomy brick stoop of his house, hating the weather. On his head he had a gray stocking cap with a black tassel. It was his grandfather's, and Moonta did not need to wear it in this mild, soggy weather, but he wore it every winter because—somehow—a warm, woolen stocking cap seemed to stand for cold and ice. As wet and damp as the weather was, and the brick stoop and all of him was, Moonta refused to budge. He sat hating the weather.

11

Lees, the neighbor woman across the street, came out of her house to shake out a rug. She looked up at the sky. Moonta on his stoop sat as quiet as in church while Lees studied the sky. Lees understood weather—every kid in the village knew that. She knew more about weather than most seamen. That was because her father had been a captain on a big boat that even went as far as America.

There—now Lees went back to the top step of her stoop and stood sniffing the weather. When Lees brought her eyes down, she saw Moonta on his stoop. "Cold, boy. Cold and nasty," Lees sang out.

"Just nasty—not cold," Moonta said shortly.

"Ah, but there's a change coming. It's going to freeze, Moonta. You're going to learn to skate before this week is out. You mark my word, by Saturday—Sunday at the latest— we'll have ice."

Something was burning or boiling over inside Lee's little house. She turned and ran. Moonta was glad she'd gone, because there he sat like a fool with hopeful tears in his eyes —just because Lees had promised ice.

With Lees gone, Moonta jumped up and stood on the top step of his stoop to sniff the higher air. But all he smelled was the sad burnt smell of Lees's buttermilk porridge. Lees came back to slam her door shut; she glared at Moonta as if he had burnt her porridge. Then, as Lees's door slammed, over the top of the dike fog came rolling out of the sea. Lees had promised

12

frost and ice, but instead fog rolled over the dike and lowered over the village. In a few minutes Moonta could not even see the dike anymore. He simply could not stand to look at the fog one moment longer. He kicked off his wooden shoes at the door, turned them upside down, and ran into the house.

There was no one home. That meant he could look at his skates without anyone knowing it. It was certainly better to play with his skates than to sit looking at a fog come rolling up out of the sea.

Moonta hurried down the hall into the living room. He climbed the chair that stood below his high closet bed built into the wall, careful not to move the chair so its legs would not punch through the newly laid linoleum where it bulged up against the wall below the closet beds. He closed the bed doors behind him so if anyone should come in, they wouldn't see him in bed in the daytime playing with his skates.

With the doors closed it was pitch-dark inside the closet bed. It didn't matter to Moonta, for he knew exactly where his skates were. He always kept them behind the black horse that stood on the shelf built above the foot end of the bed. His mother had given him the toy horse on red wheels that winter when he'd been so sick with pneumonia. But his father had given him new skates the next winter when he'd been kept in the house with a cold.

The skates were just as new as when they'd been bought, because they'd never been used. But they still fit. Father said that as fast as Moonta grew, he'd bought them plenty big enough for Moonta's feet.

The skates of course had to be strapped to your Sunday leather shoes; they couldn't be tied to wooden shoes. Moonta had never had them on under his Sunday shoes, but he knew the skates were still big enough. He often strapped them to his stockinged feet at night in bed.

If ice was really coming, the way Lees had said, he really ought to try his skates on under his shoes. Moonta let himself down from the bed to the chair, raced to the shelf at the head of the cellar stairs, raced back to the bed, and closed the doors. He found that he could tie his skates to his shoes fast—he'd practiced so often at night, tying them to his stockinged feet.

In the dark bed behind the closed doors Moonta lay back with a sigh. He couldn't see the fog come rolling over the village, and he had his skates on his feet—properly tied under his Sunday leather shoes. . . .

It seemed only the next moment, but it was really hours later, and it was awful. In all his life Moonta had never been so shamed before his father and mother—they caught him in bed in the daytime with his skates strapped to his Sunday shoes.

He'd fallen asleep! With the bed doors tightly shut he'd fallen asleep in the dark. Father and Mother had come home in the fog, they'd had tea in the living room, and all the while he'd been right there too—sleeping behind the closed bed doors.

At last Mother had got worried because he wasn't home. She'd gone through the thick fog to Grandfather's house, only to find that Moonta hadn't been there at all. After that they'd all gone out to look for him, worried sick. His mother had looked through the village, Father had gone along the deep ditches on both sides of every road that led out of the village. Grandfather had gone far out along the canal.

All the time Moonta had known nothing of it; he'd gone on sleeping in the bed behind the closed doors.

Mother found him. When Mother jerked open the two bed doors, he jerked awake. He lay mute with shame. There was

15

nothing to say. There he lay before his mother—in the full light that the lamp above the table shed into the closet bed —full length on top of the covers with shoes on, and skates tied to the shoes.

"You!" Mother cried. "There you lie—and if it hadn't been you'd snored, we'd never have found you. Who'd think to look for a big boy like you in a bed in the daytime?"

At first he was so confused and groggy with sleep, he couldn't get things straight. The light shone hard in his eyes. "Children don't snore," he told Mother groggily and sleepily.

"Everybody snores," Mother said. "Well, if you didn't snore, at least you sort of snorkeled. And you were threshing your feet in some dream."

Mother's eyes went wide, then her mouth fell open as if she couldn't find words—she just pointed where her eyes were looking. "And me arguing about snoring," she cried. "Look at that quilt. My best quilt ripped and torn and cut and . . . and look at you. Shoes on. Skates on. Skates on in bed!"

At that awful moment Father threw open the outer door and yelled down the hall: "Is Moonta here? Because if he isn't, I'm going to get them to ring the alarm bell in the tower, so the whole village can go out with lanterns. You can't see a hand before your eyes anymore. I took his grandfather home for fear the old man would walk into the canal."

"No, he's here," Mother wailed. "Oh, he's here, I just now found him. Come and look, or you'll never believe it. He was

16

here all the time—asleep in bed—with shoes and skates on!"

Moonta heard Father come clattering down the hall on his wooden shoes. For the first time in his life his father must have dashed right in without first knocking off his wooden shoes. And Mother was too upset to notice. As Father turned into the doorway of the living room Moonta pushed himself over the edge and jumped down from the high bed. He didn't think of the skates on his feet. The skates sliced through the bulged linoleum like a knife slicing through bologna, except that there was a tearing sound. It was awful—there he had to stand before Father and Mother, his skates caught in the sticky new linoleum where it bulged up against the wall with the beds.

"My brand-new linoleum!" Mother sounded as if she were weeping every word.

"Oh," Moonta mumbled, "I forgot." He stood, shamed and miserable, looking down at his feet.

Father sat down on the nearest chair, the wet wooden shoes still on his feet, and looked puzzled. "How does a sane, normal mortal come to think up things like that—skates and shoes on in bed? Now why—can you just tell me reasonably— why did you put skates on to go to bed?"

"Lees said cold and ice were coming," Moonta told Father earnestly and honestly. "And then I thought of my skates, and then I tried them on my Sunday shoes to see if they were still big enough, and then, I guess, I fell asleep. . . ." Then after all

17

those "and then's" there was suddenly nothing more to say.

Father got up and went to the front door. He threw it open and left it open. The fog actually came rolling up the long hall and into the living room. Father stood among the wisps of fog floating in through the living room doorway. "Look," he said, "this is fog. It's thick, but you can't skate on fog. So Lees promised you ice. Lees! Lees is a seamstress, and she sits all day in a closed room, stooped over a sewing machine. . . ."

"Oh, but all the kids say that Lees . . ." Moonta didn't finish. It would sound pretty silly to talk about Lees knowing all about weather—with a fog drifting in through the living room door.

Thank goodness. Father went to close the front door. When he came back this time, he had remembered to take off his wooden shoes. "All right," Father said. "You gave us a couple of horrible hours, worrying and searching. You've cut the linoleum, you cut up a quilt. Well, you put yourself to bed with your skates on, now I'm putting you to bed without skates, and without any supper."

He grabbed Moonta under the arms, lifted and pulled until with a dull plop the linoleum let go of the skate runners. He set Moonta on the edge of the high bed, ripped off his skates and shoes, pulled off his clothes, and pushed him flat on the bed. Then he said, "If you've got to be childish, let's make it real childish." He climbed the chair, reached over and took down the black horse with the red wheels, and shoved it into Moonta's hands. "There, now lie and play with that."

There Moonta had to lie, the bed doors wide open, the lamplight bright in the bed, holding his toy horse in his hands. He didn't dare put the horse down, didn't dare push it out of sight under the quilts. He obediently, foolishly held it. But he didn't look at it.

Mother went into the kitchen in the silence. Later there came the odors of food as Mother cooked a late supper for herself and Father. Still later Mother brought the steaming food into the room and set it on the table. There Moonta lay with the lovely rolls of steam coming over him in the cooped bed, almost the way the fog had come wisping through the doorway. It made him ravenously hungry. But all he could think to do was to press his nose into the woolly fur of the little black horse to shut out the heavenly odors.

Everybody was unhappy and silent in the room. There was nothing but the noise of forks and knives. Moonta couldn't stand it. He turned his eyes away, turned his back, but he obediently kept holding the little black horse.

Right after their belated supper Father and Mother had to go practice singing in the village choir. Before she left, Mother came to the bed to see if Moonta was properly tucked in. She worked with the pillow, but Moonta did not turn around.

When they were gone, Moonta smelled food, and then he found that Mother had secretly tucked a smoked eel sandwich in a flat, covered dish under his pillow. Smoked eel! Mother was that way. He wolfed the delicious sandwich gratefully.

19

But when he got on his knees to set the dish on the foot-end shelf, Moonta also put the horse back in its place. Only then did he notice that Father had taken his skates away. The skates were gone, and somehow the whole shelf seemed empty—the skates had lain there so many years. Well, he didn't need the skates, all there was was fog anyway. But the horse with red wheels was back where it belonged. Moonta lay back contentedly and licked at the lovely smoked eel taste on his ten fingertips.

He felt immensely relieved now that the little horse was back in its place on the shelf. Father shouldn't have done that —made him feel silly and babyish, holding it. It belonged on the shelf with the bright skates behind it. Somehow the shelf stayed seemingly empty, but the woolly, fuzzy, curly-haired horse was back where it belonged.

Everybody called him a roughneck, and Moonta wouldn't for all the world have any of the other kids know that he still kept his toy horse. Imagine, he'd only been four years old when Mother had given him the horse because he was so sick with pneumonia. But always, still it seemed as if clinging to the fuzzy black horse had brought him through the awful fevers of that sickness.

Of course he knew it wasn't really so; it was the doctor, and the minister praying for him in church, and all that. . . . But mostly it was Mother sitting up with him night and day. Of course Father had sat up with him too, to relieve Mother for a few hours of sleep. There had been good ice all those sick weeks of that winter, too, but Father and Mother hadn't gone skating at all—even though they were champions.

Somehow the little black horse seemed to stand for all that, and that's why it had to stand in the selfsame place on the shelf where it had stood whenever he had been too sick with pneumonia to hold it. Of course Father didn't know—maybe even Mother didn't—and he couldn't have explained to them why the little horse belonged.

But the skates belonged too—behind the black horse on the bed shelf. Father had bought the skates, he'd said, for a big hope for Moonta that the next winter of ice he surely would learn to skate.

Yes, the skates too had to be back on the shelf, for a big hope still that this winter there surely would be ice.

2

Great Day in the Afternoon

WEDNESDAY was a great day. Thus far it seemed to be about the greatest day in Moonta's whole life. Wednesday was a great day simply because it was cold at last. It still wasn't bitter cold or freezing cold, just windy, blustery cold. But cold!

It had stormed all through the night. It had stormed so hard that often Moonta had lain awake listening. And the storm had blown the three-day fog back out into the sea. That was the first and most important thing. Because no ice could come when there was a fog.

22

Wednesday was a free afternoon from school. It wasn't going to be very free for Moonta—just busy and wonderful. Wednesday afternoons Father always cleaned out his carpenter shop, and Moonta had to help. It was his job to sweep up the sawdust and shavings from the whole shop, then carry them by the basketful behind the dike to burn them at the edge of the sea.

Never had Moonta felt so willing. He felt so good, so hopeful in the raw, windy cold, he'd have been willing to do anything.

Neither Father nor Mother seemed to think anything of it that it had turned cold, just as Lees had said it would. At least they didn't say anything about it. Mother was even washing clothes this cold, raw, windy afternoon.

In the carpenter shop Moonta waited only long enough to fill the first basket full of shavings. He stamped them down. Father was up in the loft straightening the lumber piles he kept there.

"First basketful ready," Moonta called up to the loft. Then he rushed off to the dike with the basket. He'd hardly dumped the shavings in a small pile at the foot of the dike when Father came over the dike with an even bigger basket of shavings. He dumped it on top of Moonta's pile. That helped, because the wind came sweeping down the dike so rough and blustery, it was blowing Moonta's piled shavings away. Father pulled the sheet of blackened metal out of the bottom of his big basket. "You know what to do," he said with a secretive wink and a grin.

Moonta ran off and gathered handfuls of mussels and clams along the dike pilings. When he came back he threw them on top of the metal sheet on the fire.

The raw, rough wind sweeping down the dike made it such a roaring hot fire, the mussels and clams were done in no time. The shells opened, and as fast as they could, Moonta and Father ate the delicious hot morsels.

He and his father always did it—every Wednesday afternoon. It was a secret between them, because the villagers despised mussels and clams; they'd rather starve than eat them. Only Moonta and his father seemed to know how marvelously delicious they really were. But everybody else would have thought it disgusting. It was a long-time secret just between him and his father—even Mother didn't know about it.

"*Mmmm,*" Father said, licking his fingers. "Makes you want to clean out the shop every day. Is there anything as good in the whole wide world? Hey, gather some more, and I'll see if I can scrape up some more shavings—even if I have to make them first."

Father came over the dike with the new basket of shavings. "Did you gather some more you-know-what?" he called down the dike. Moonta held up his basket. The bottom was covered with mussels and clams.

Just then a big gust of wind came along the dike and swept Father's whole basket clean of all its shavings. They blew feathery high into the air, fell down on the dike, and blew out over the village—a small, yellow-shavings snowstorm.

Father laughed as he watched it. "I guess that must be Lees's snowstorm that she predicted. Or was it ice? Well, I must say for Lees that the weather did change. This wind is really getting rough and cold. I've got to give Lees credit—I

25

wouldn't be surprised now if the real cold doesn't fall into the place left by this wind and last night's storm."

Moonta stood stock-still. Now even Father admitted that it had turned cold. But Lees had said it three days ago. Moonta didn't know what to say. If it had been another kid, he would have yelled up the dike, "Yeah, cold; but you said Lees didn't know about weather—just about sewing machines." Of course you couldn't yell anything like that to your father, or to any grown-up. All the kids knew it about Lees, but grown-ups just didn't seem to believe until things actually came.

Father looked around far out to sea. Then he peered into his empty basket again. "Well, no more of you-know-what, on account of no more shavings. Better tuck *them* all away between the pilings for next Wednesday, for Wednesday always comes again, and it's better than the Queen's birthday." Father laughed and with his blown-empty basket went back down the dike.

With the carpenter shop all swept, the cold that had come after the storm gave Moonta something else to do. He still had to find his skates. Father had really hidden them. Three days now, and Moonta hadn't found them anywhere in the house, nor in Grandpa's barn, nor today in the carpenter shop. About the only place left to look was up in the attic.

This afternoon, with Mother in the yard hanging up the

washing, would give him a swell chance to sneak into the attic and hunt without her knowing.

Maybe now at last ice was coming, but even if it didn't come, it just seemed the shiny skates had to be on the bed shelf back of the little horse. Moonta felt sure he could explain to his father why it had to be that way—sure now that it was so good and cold, that even if he explained it badly Father would understand.

Up in the attic Moonta first searched the bed because that would be the quietest. Mother hadn't seen him going up to the attic, so he must be very quiet. The attic bed wasn't high like the downstairs closet beds. It had to be low because it had been squeezed in under the slant of the roof. Moonta thought that the real reason he searched there first was because he'd always liked the open, narrow bunk bed. It had no doors. The bed in the high, lone attic right under the red tile of the roof was, well, sort of like a secret nest in a tree. He'd often begged Mother, but she'd never yet let him sleep up here. "I have to know what you're up to, even at night," she always said. "Because you're usually up to something."

Moonta again reminded himself to be careful when he searched through the stacked piles of discarded things against the end wall of the attic—nothing must tumble and clatter to the floor. He searched and he searched, but nowhere did he find his skates. Suddenly he had to stand very still. Mother had come into the house. She was in the kitchen right under him. He could hear her singing to herself.

Then as Moonta stood there without a sound, he found himself listening more to the wind on the roof tiles above him than to Mother down below. It was very secret, and very hopeful, listening to the wind. Little squiggles of happy hope kept writhing all through him. It was hard to be still. Father's saying this afternoon on the dike that the real cold might fall into the place left by the storm made everything hopeful. Somehow it made it seem ten times as sure as Lees saying it— even though Lees was the weather prophet. And after the cold, ice should come. Lees had said it three days ago, but now that Father was saying it too, it seemed to make it so.

Oh, the ice wouldn't come while the wind was still blowing and the sea storming. Ice came only in stillness. The real hard, bearing-down cold came over the water only after stiff, cold days and long, still nights. The stiller the day, the stiller the night, the stiller the water, the sooner the ice came, and the thicker it grew. Moonta knew that all he had to do was to wait for the stillness to come.

Here, up in the attic, inside the silence of the four walls, you could tell that the storm was going. The wind hadn't by any means all gone out to sea, the wind still came slamming down on the red roof tiles over his head. But it didn't last anymore. Between the hard, rough slammings little silences and hopeful waits would come into the wind. Then the wind would come again. It would pipe and sigh over the top of the roof tiles, with sly wind-whisperings.

The next moment, just as suddenly, it would bellow along the roof, bluster and howl tied-wild-beast howls down the wide chimney, scream and shriek up from the roof tiles. The very next moment the wind would begin its little bad-boy-being-good sly whisperings again.

Carefully, so Mother wouldn't hear, Moonta crossed the length of the attic to the lone, small window in the far wall.

Theirs was a high attic, higher than the dike, higher than the low roofs of the other houses. Not only could Moonta look down on the low roofs of the other houses, he could look over them down on the square field behind the village with its network of crisscrossing drainage ditches. If ice came after this cold, that's where the ice would come first—to those ditches. It always did, it always had. That is why, way back in history, they had made that field a village community field and called it the Children's Skate School Field. From times out of mind that field was where the children of the village had learned to skate. But once they could skate without falling and stumbling and windmilling their arms, then, proudly, they might come to skate with the grown-ups of the whole village on the canal.

Moonta sighed. Big as he was, nine years old and going on ten, and in the fourth grade, if ice came, that was where he

29

would have to learn too. On the ditches with all the littlest kids. Moonta quietly slipped the window open to see the field better.

The cold wind slammed at him. Oh, it was cold here—why, it was, it must be, even colder here than down in the Skate School Field, even if ice did come there first. But did it? Of course he didn't know; you looked for ice in ditches, not up in an attic.

Suddenly Moonta was struck by a great idea. He closed the window softly, backed over, and sat on the edge of the bed to think it out. First he admitted that the real reason he kept worrying about the Skate School Field was because he was ashamed, big as he was, to have to learn with the littlest kids. That was why already twice this cold day he'd run out there. He wanted to be the first one to know when the ice was safe in the ditches. In the hope that if he knew first, he could practice skating first, and all alone. In the big hope that he could learn before the little kids. In the almost desperate hope that he'd learn well enough before anyone else started skating, so that then, when ice came to the canal, he could move to the canal with all the big fifth and sixth graders and the grown-ups of the village.

Now the cold wind slamming at the high window had given Moonta the idea by which he could be the first to know that ice had come. Why, all he'd have to do was to set a shallow pan of water in the attic window sill and watch it. Now he could rush downstairs and give Mother a good reason why he was in the attic.

When Moonta opened the door of the stairway, Mother was in the kitchen ironing. She whirled around. "Moonta, you know you shouldn't be up in that cold attic. Do you want to be sick again? What were you doing up there?"

"Mother," Moonta said hastily, "may I go to Grandpa's barn—"

She didn't let him finish. "What," she said, "and run out to the Skate School Field again, along all those ditches? They've told me you were messing around there twice today, and I've told you again and again, I don't want you playing along those ditches. What if you'd fall in and get wet and get sick again?"

"I wasn't going there," Moonta said disgustedly. "I was going to Grandpa's barn to get a shallow dishpan he used to use for his chickens. Mother, may I put it in the attic window and put water in it—so I'll know the first thing when there's ice?"

"What if it blew out of that high window and landed on somebody's head?" Mother asked doubtfully.

"I'll put a big stone in it," Moonta said.

Mother was eying her ironing, her mind going back to her work. "Oh, all right, restless rustle-pants, but don't go near those ditches . . . and come right back. I declare, if we don't get ice soon, there won't be any living with you."

31

She started ironing, and on tiptoe Moonta crossed behind her and shot out of the kitchen door. Then he ran hard—she so often called him back to put on more clothes, or to do this or that.

Moonta emerged from Grandfather's barn with the old banged-up dishpan just as Grandfather came toward the barn door.

"Grandpa, may I have this old pan to put water in so I can tell as soon as there is ice?" he asked.

He had to explain it all over again. It didn't make sense to Grandpa.

Grandpa stood marveling and shaking his head. "Do you ever think about anything but ice?" he asked. Then he said, "Well, if ice is that important to you, go ahead with your ice studies."

Moonta whirled away. "Mother said I had to come straight back home," he called over his shoulder by way of excuse for his abruptness. "Thank you, Grandpa."

Grandpa still stood there. "Well, all I can say, Moonta, is that if ice doesn't come soon, your parents had better move with you to Nova Zembla or Outer Siberia. I hear there's plenty of ice there—all the time."

Moonta laughed loudly as he ran on, to show Grandpa it was a good joke.

But Grandpa called out suddenly, "Oh, in case you were

snooping in my barn to find your skates, I can tell you they're not there."

Moonta stopped. "I wasn't snooping," he called back indignantly. The truth was he'd been so full of his dishpan plan, he'd forgotten about his skates. "Then where are they?" he asked.

"I wouldn't know," Grandpa said innocently. "For all I know they're in Outer Siberia."

Grandpa was joking again. Moonta ran on.

3

Frost and Flounders

NOW there was going to be ice. Lees had predicted there'd be ice by the end of the week—Sunday at the latest—and here it was only Thursday afternoon. Sometime Wednesday night the wind had stopped blowing, and the stillness had come— the stillness needed to make ice. Why, your breath plumed out of your mouth, and when you stood still it rose straight up, like gray smoke out of a chimney. When your breath did that it meant still air. And still air meant frost and ice.

Moonta was running home from school. But every once in a while he stopped, stood perfectly still to watch his breath in the cold air, then dashed on again.

Moonta flung into the house. Luckily Mother wasn't in the kitchen, so he could kick off his wooden shoes and race up to the attic. He heard Mother call out a quick question from the living room, but that didn't stop him; it only made him go plunging up two steps at a time.

Now Mother was at the foot of the attic stairway, but he could pay no attention. Even through the attic window he could see it—ice in the pan in the window sill. Solid ice. Of course there'd been hardly more than a film of water in the pan. The wind Wednesday night had blown most of it out, but now, there it stood—solid ice around the big stone.

Mother was still at the foot of the stairs, asking all kinds of questions and demanding answers. He whirled, and hurled himself down the stairway straight at her. She actually backed away.

"Mother, Mother," he yelled, "ice in the pan! Ice! Now may I go play in Grandpa's barn?"

It didn't fool Mother a moment; she knew exactly what he was going to do. "I've told you—I don't want you messing around alone in that field, with all those ditches full of water. Don't you realize how I worry?"

"Mother, there's ice in the pan, not water," he said indignantly.

"So there's a smidgen of ice in that shallow pan. That doesn't mean there'll be ice on the ditches. So it's gotten cold, but you've said yourself there can't be any ice this soon."

Moonta dismally had to admit that he knew it. Sometimes

he just babbled too much to Mother. . . . Now he could think of no good argument to persuade her to let him go—ice or no ice. He spread his hands hopelessly wide. "But, Mother," he said, "school's out, and there's still the whole rest of the afternoon; and even if there is no ice on the ditches, I'd much rather go look for nothing than to do nothing."

Mother dropped her hands helplessly. "You can always find an argument faster than I can," she said. "Oh, go ahead. Otherwise you'll be impossible all evening. But watch yourself. And listen, Moonta, it's no use snooping in Grandfather's barn again—your skates aren't there."

"Oh, I hadn't even thought of it," Moonta said innocently. "And anyway, Grandpa said my skates were in Outer Siberia."

Mother didn't laugh at Grandfather's joke. "I'm a fool to let you go," she said worriedly. "Just remember, you don't actually have to stand at the very edges of those muddy, slippery ditches."

"Oh, I won't, I won't," Moonta promised fervently. He walked very sedately to the door to show Mother he was calm and careful. He even forced himself to take time about shoving his feet into his wooden shoes. He closed the door softly, then he flew.

There was ice in the Children's Skate School Field. Moonta had found a ditch— Well, it wasn't really a ditch—just a sort of a long, shallow hole in among marsh grass. Moonta had

gone far back in the field, as far away from the village as possible, so no one could see exactly what he was doing; and
there in a shallow pool of water he'd found ice.

It wasn't really, truly fair, he had to admit. The water hole
was too shallow. And it wasn't covered with ice; the ice was
just beginning to finger out from the grassy edges. Long, thin
slivers of ice poked from the edges toward the middle. But it
did mean it was freezing. At last it was truly, genuinely
freezing.

Moonta searched around for a pebble to test one of the
many thin, slivery fingers of ice. He couldn't find a single
stone in the grass. Impatiently he poked in his pocket for
something. It would be that this once he had absolutely nothing in his pockets. Well, nothing but a safety pin Mother had
put in to close a hole until she could sew it shut tonight when
he was in bed. He pulled the pocket inside out and took out
the pin. He'd put it back after he had tested the ice. It wasn't
very heavy, but it was better than nothing. He got down on
hands and knees, then he dropped the closed safety pin on
one of the ice fingers. To his dismay the pin fell right through;
it didn't even hesitate. But there was a hole that the pin had
made. So it was ice, it wasn't just a film of scum.

The pin was gone, but Moonta joyfully brushed off his
damp knees. Then he went whistling through the field, making believe he was pegging imaginary stones at imaginary
birds so no one that saw him would guess what he was really

37

doing. But wherever he searched through the field there wasn't any more ice. There wasn't a sliver or a beginning of ice on any of the ditches, but that was because they were deeper and were drainage ditches. The current might be so slight and slow you couldn't see it with your eyes, but still that little movement in the water would be enough to slow up the freezing. Tonight, Moonta assured himself, tonight it'll start.

He stood absolutely still and watched the breath pluming out of his mouth, straight up before his face, straight up as if going to heaven and God. It seemed to him that his pluming breath was almost like a prayer going up to God, saying: "Please, God, make ice—make it fast."

It seemed so like a prayer, he just had to circle back to the water hole to see if his prayer had been answered. When he got to the water hole, it seemed sure there was more ice and that the ice fingers were longer.

Moonta searched hard along the water hole, but all he could find was a tiny snail shell. He made himself believe it was heavier than the safety pin, but it really wasn't, for when he dropped it on the very same finger of ice it didn't go through. The little shell bounced and skittered along the finger of ice until it slid into the water. Moonta kneeled there and looked, and a tuneless humming of pure joy rose in him. It didn't stop until he became aware that one hand was resting right on a little pebble in the grass.

A pebble was a stone, and a stone was heavy. Moonta hardly dared test the finger of ice with it. If it went right through . . . He chose another ice finger that looked thicker than the one on which he had dropped the small shell. He cheated a little. He bent down, and did not hold his hand as far from the ice. He dropped the pebble. It stayed where it landed—it sank into the ice but it didn't go through. The ice was holding the pebble. Moonta would not stay to watch the pebble sink through the ice. He wiped off both soggy knees with his woolen cap, then ran for home as hard as he could.

In the hall, where no one could see him, Moonta skipped and danced all the long way down to the kitchen. He was relieved that Mother was frying sputtering fish in the kitchen, so she couldn't possibly have heard him acting like a four-year-old all the way down the hall. To cover up his embarrassment he came slowly into the kitchen, took off his stocking cap, and stood looking into it.

Mother turned around. "What solemn depths of thought," she said. "Are those all coming out of your cap?"

"It's freezing," Moonta announced seriously. "It's making ice—a little bit." Then he rushed out what he wanted to ask. "Mother, may I put more water in the pan in the window-sill to see how deep it'll freeze in the night? And . . . and, Mother, may I sleep in the bed up in the attic tonight? If it's going to freeze, I want to be near it, right under the roof, right under the sky."

"Well, all right," she said, "but just tonight. If ice means that much to you, and of course you've been waiting for it so long, then, yes, just for tonight."

If Mother hadn't been at the stove frying fish, he'd have hugged her, but it was awkward to hug from behind.

"Just so you don't get your hopes up too high," Mother was saying. "You'll be so disappointed. We've had it so often, Moonta, bits and dribbles of thin ice. Then when you turn around there's a thaw, and it's gone again. Try to keep calm."

Mother's words filled Moonta with consternation. He'd never thought of that—a sudden change in the weather, a sudden thaw. He stood troubled. "Mother, may I take Lees a fried fish?" he asked abruptly.

"Oh, for a bribe?" Mother teased. "A fish, so Lees will promise you tons of ice, at least a foot thick—and no thaw?" But she was just joking, for she promptly scooped three small, sputtering flounders from the pan into a dish. "Here, then, not just one, the three best and tenderest fish for Lees. That ought to produce the fiercest freezing weather and the thickest ice."

Moonta was in no mood for jokes. He carried the platter with the three fish solemnly, stiffly before him. Lees knew the weather—even if Father and Mother didn't want to believe it and made jokes about it. Still, he didn't feel quite sure now after Mother's jokes. What if Lees would promise hard freezing weather just because of the fish?

Across the street, Moonta shoved the top door open and

yelled down the hall to let Lees know she had company. When Lees came bustling down the hall, before she could possibly smell the fried fish, Moonta called out: "Lees, is it really going to freeze? There's no thaw coming, is there, Lees?"

"No, but there's fish coming," Lees said, and Moonta could hear her sniffing in the long, dark hall. "Oh, there's fish coming—and who can fry fish like your mother?"

Moonta did not go into Lees's house with the platter; he wanted her to come out on her stoop and sniff the air. Lees did. She sniffed all around. "If you ask me, right tonight— right this very night—we're going to get a frost that'll make the brick of your house crack and crackle . . . and me with no turf in my bin, and the turf boat, slow as it is, will be frozen tight into the ice on the canal long before it can possibly get to our village. . . . Well, I'm afraid, Moonta, you'll have a frozen neighbor woman by morning—frozen right in her bed —but at least she'll be full of good fish."

Moonta started to laugh, but then he just stared at Lees with his mouth open. Now this couldn't be—Lees wouldn't promise all that for just three little fish. "Really, truly?" he asked Lees. He almost didn't dare—after all, Lees was a grown-up—but he had to know. "Honest, Lees, cross your heart?"

"Cross my heart, and hope to die, and whatever more goes with it," Lees solemnly promised. "I could tell better if I wasn't sniffing these delicious fish odors at the same time . . .

but try it yourself, Moonta. Take a deep sniff—up from your toes."

Moonta did. Then he had to grab the bridge of his nose, it hurt and tingled. The next moment his nose started to feel like wood.

Lees rubbed the bridge of her own long nose. "Hurts, doesn't it? Well, that means a deep, hard frost, the air's that crackling sharp. Better tuck down under the covers tonight, Moonta. Don't freeze your ears."

If it hadn't been for the platter of fish, he would have hugged Lees. He galloped away to his own house. Before he closed the outer door he drew a deep breath up from his toes, and this time it seemed to hurt even more. He had to hold his nose all the way down the hall, but he yelled out, "Mother, have we got plenty of turf? Mother, may I take Lees some of ours, because the turf boat is going to freeze in the ice. . . ."

He stopped in the kitchen doorway. The turf boat freeze in the ice? Even he couldn't believe that.

Mother wasn't in the kitchen, but on the table there was a hot, fried flounder on a plate and a note beside it. "Had to run out to the store to get more green oil to fry the fish. Don't eat more than this small one. I don't want you to spoil your appetite for supper."

Right then he could have eaten ten flounders and not spoiled his appetite. Right then he couldn't have spoiled anything, everything was perfect. He loved the flounder, he loved Mother and Lees, but most of all, he loved the big frost that was going to crack down over the land and water in the long, big stillness of the night.

He sat down to his flounder, then he jumped up again. What if Father and Mother just laughed about Lees's needing turf in the coming night's cold? They hadn't believed Lees before the fog. What if they just laughed about the turf boat freezing in the ice?

He ran to the turf bin behind the kitchen. The long turfs stacked in the bin looked like long loaves of square sandwich bread—of course, sooty black. There was a whole new pile that hadn't been touched yet stacked up against the back of the bin. But right before his feet was a last little pile of about seven turfs. He decided he'd take those to Lees—he'd tell Mother about it afterward. He grabbed a burlap bag off a hook and laid it over his sleeve so he could pile the turf on his arm without getting all black.

Then when he picked up the two top ones, the turf in the middle of the pile of seven wasn't a turf at all, it was a black shoe box, almost the size of the thick turf. Even before he opened it he knew that there were his skates. He peeked inside, and there they lay—side by side in the black box— clean and new, and bright as ever. Imagine, he never would have found them if he hadn't decided to take the turfs to Lees.

Man, oh, man, everything had certainly turned out perfectly this day. Now he even had skates—and Lees would

44

have turf. Why, he could sleep up in the attic tonight with his skates. But he mustn't forget to fill the dishpan with water up to its rim. Somehow because of it all, it seemed sure that it was going to freeze hard tonight—so hard you could hear it crackle.

Now it really seemed that the pluming breath of his prayer in the Skate School Field *had* gone straight up to God. The day, he thought, was solemn with goodness. "Make it freeze, make it freeze," he said aloud to the stars as he crossed the street with his turf.

4

The Whole New World

IT WAS Father who was shaking Moonta in the middle of the night. It wasn't dark; there was a pale, cold light falling through the open attic window.

For a sleepy moment as he wakened, Moonta had been scared of his father, looming over him in the bed. His father's dark mustache had sparkled and shone in the light of the oil lamp he had held up beside his face. The attic had not needed the lamplight. Now Father blew it out and set the lamp on the floor. Even in his waking scare Moonta somehow realized it was ice in Father's mustache.

46

Then, as Father hurriedly slung him over his shoulder, the round ball tassel of Moonta's sleeping cap whipped up and over and hit Moonta on the nose. It hurt! It was hard. It was hard because the woolly ball of a tassel had become a ball of ice. Even Father must have heard it clunk, because he grabbed and felt the tassel. "Well, I'll be . . ." he said loudly in the hollow attic. "It's frozen solid. Of all nights for you to pick to sleep in the attic. Why didn't you just sleep on top of the dike? What a frost this must be."

As Father said the words, his teeth chattering, Moonta could see the breath stutter-puff out of his mouth with every word. Father started across the attic on a run, but Moonta begged. "The pan. The pan in the window!"

Father made disgusted, impatient sounds, but he did turn toward the window. And there in the clear, frosty light of the night stood the pan, frozen solid.

Father rammed the window shut. "You with the window open on a night like this. What a night for your mother to give in to your silliness and let you sleep here. But how could she know you'd sleep with the window wide open?"

"I was going to watch it all through the night—every once in a while—but I guess I just slept," Moonta said. "It's solid —solid with ice."

"I'm just amazed you're not solid with ice, even under all those covers," Father said as he raced down the attic stairs.

47

When they burst into the living room Mother woke fuzzily. "Oh, he's awake," she muttered from the bed.

"Well, he ought to be," Father said. "I nearly knocked his brains out with the tassel of his own cap. It was frozen hard. Look at my mustache. It's a wonder he didn't freeze us all to death. He had that attic window wide open."

"No!" Mother said. But she didn't seem to be wide-awake. "He'd better sleep between us, then—if he's that cold." She fumbled with the covers, moved over, and made room. She held out her arms.

It made Moonta feel a bit silly and babyish to sleep between his parents like a three-year-old. But he couldn't think much about it; all he could think of was the solid ice in the pan. The next moment he was glad of the warmth of the bed and of Mother. He was rigid with cold.

He lay shivering, snuggled against Mother, and then he noticed that his father had left the room. Father came back, tiptoeing gingerly over the icy linoleum. He had a long turf in each hand. He shoved them into the stove, poked and rattled around until there was a little glow and a little flame. "Glad it didn't go out entirely," he heard Father mutter. "With him having that window open it'll be like trying to heat the North Sea."

"Is it that bad?" Mother murmured along Moonta's ear.

"That bad?" Father said disgustedly as he came on a tiptoe run from the stove and made a flying leap for the high closet bed. "I don't remember a cold snap coming this fast and hitting this hard in all my life."

"Grandpa said in eighteen ninety-two," Moonta announced. "It came, Grandpa said, all in one night and it stayed all winter. You know what Grandpa said? People actually got sick of ice that winter, it stayed so long."

"Eighteen ninety-two, huh?" Father said, amused. "Well, Grandpa'd know, and you'd remember, if it had anything to do with ice. Hope you're that good with your dates in history in school."

Moonta hardly heard Father, for he'd been thinking. "Oh, I'm glad now," he blurted out, "that I took Lees those turfs . . . " he caught himself. "I just took them off the big new pile," he said hastily. "Mother was at the store, so I couldn't ask, and Lees said the turf boat would freeze in the ice on the canal tonight."

"What?" Father said. "Did Lees predict this hard a frost?" He made noises. "No," he said, "a seamstress sitting hunched over a sewing machine." But he did not sound unbelieving now.

"I was thinking," Mother said, "the china teapot on the kitchen table right in front of the window—I didn't empty it last night. Could it crack?"

"With the attic window and the stairway door wide open, it could," Father said unwillingly. "But let it crack. If I get any colder, I'll crack."

49

"Let me," Moonta begged. "Father's feet are so cold now, they feel like stones."

He didn't wait. He crawled over Father, let himself hang from the edge of the bed, and dropped to the floor. He gasped. The linoleum was so hard cold, it felt more like ice than ice did. He raced to the kitchen and emptied the teapot. Hoping his bare feet wouldn't make too much noise, he scooted up to the attic and grabbed the skates from under the covers. The skates just had to be back on the shelf of his own bed, now with ice coming.

He hurried back to the living room and begged, "May I sleep in my own bed?"

"What's the matter?" Father asked. "Feel too big to sleep with your folks?"

Moonta nodded. But Mother said, "It isn't that—he's holding something behind his back. He must have found his skates when he took turf to Lees, and now that there's going to be ice, he wants to sleep with his skates." Mother was certainly wide-awake now.

It was so right, Moonta could only nod up at his father. "Well," Father said, "if he prefers ice-cold, hard skates to soft, warm me . . . guess it's all right. I was going to give them to him in the morning anyway. Don't sneak out in the night, though, and go skating, Moonta."

"Oh, no," Moonta said, aghast. He looked in consternation at Father until he saw his father wink. Then he flew, slid a chair across the icy linoleum, opened the bed doors, and flung himself up into his bed. In bed he laid the skates back in their place behind the little black horse. He lay there bone-cold and shivering. A cold, harsh light came through the slits of the shutters and through the frosted, flowered windows. The whole room seemed to glitter, even the blades of his skates glinted and shone behind the black horse. A small warmth rose up from the stove, and suddenly Moonta felt so snug he couldn't keep awake—not even to admire the glittering skates.

Moonta wakened in the early, cold morning. His father and mother were snoring in a sort of off-key unison. Listening carefully to the breathing from the next bed, he soundlessly knotted the ends of the round leather thongs of his skates together and hung them over his shoulder. He crawled from under the warm covers and kneeled at the edge of the bed, listening long, fearful moments before he dared let himself drop to the floor. He gasped out loud as he hit the linoleum—it was like falling into ice water. He made himself stand there, listening. All his sweet, enveloping bed warmth was gone in a moment. His teeth started chattering.

Mother's breathing changed. But she only muttered and turned over. On timid, tall toes Moonta stole out of the room.

In the hall Moonta gasped in dismay. The stove with its turf must have warmed the living room a little, but here

51

stood the cold of the whole long night. The hall window had
no shutter, but Moonta could see nothing through the thick,
frosted window. Still, there was a different light coming
through the window. It must be daylight.

In the frozen hall every step on the linoleum seemed to
make the boards underneath screak and squeak—it almost
seemed the slower he stole on tiptoe, the more noise he made.
And now his feet were too numb with cold to be careful—they
were getting stumbly. In desperation Moonta at last just
flung himself down the rest of the hall and raced up the
attic stairs for his clothes. He shivered and shook so hard
he could hardly get them on.

While he dressed he kept his eyes on the attic window,
but here too he was enclosed in a secret, frozen little world.
The frost had flowered the window so thickly he could see
nothing, not even the dishpan with ice. But there must be
ice! There must even be ice on the ditches of the Children's
Skate School Field. Moonta tried to tug the window open,
but it had frozen tight since Father had slammed it shut
last night.

Moonta took time to snatch a woolen scarf and a thick
woolen sweater out of the attic cabinet where Mother kept
all their winter clothes. But no matter how he dug among
the boxes on the floor of the cabinet, he couldn't find his
mittens.

He gave up, and gave a tug at the sleeve of his sweater.

52

That's what he'd do—he'd pull his sweater sleeves way over his knuckles.

Moonta made the long, slow descent to the kitchen while every tread in the attic stairway squealed out. He started to slip out by the kitchen door. His wooden shoes standing there reminded him that he needed his Sunday leather shoes for skating—wooden shoes were no good. He had to turn back, make his way to the cellar, and open that door.

On the top step Moonta put on his leather shoes in mouse-like quietness. But when he started toward the kitchen, the shoes squeaked out at each step. It was worse than the creak of the frosty floor boards. Then Moonta stopped dead-still— Mother had called out in a soft voice from the living room.

It took him helpless, breathless moments to realize that Mother had called out in her sleep. He didn't dare risk the squeak of his shoes one other step. There was nothing to do but crawl toward the kitchen door. But when he dropped down, the skates slung around his neck hit the floor with a hard metallic clatter. For still, long, dead moments Moonta crouched over the fallen skates, hoping against hope. This time Mother did not call out, and that was even worse. Now he had no way of knowing if she had wakened and was lying there listening for his next sound.

At last it was too much, nobody could stay quiet that long. Moonta pushed back on his haunches, fumbled at his sweater, unbuttoned it, and shoved the skates up under it. But his fumbling fingers had ripped all the buttons loose, the buttons of his blouse, and even of his underwear. When he shoved his skates into the gaping opening, they struck right against his warm stomach. He couldn't help it, he squealed out at the cold touch, and then he nervously giggled.

Now he was so desperate he just buttoned a couple of buttons of the sweater over the skates and crawled away. He pulled himself up by the doorknob and softly opened the kitchen door. Suddenly he didn't care. He pulled the door shut and ran headlong through the yard into the cobblestone street—anything to get out of sight and hearing of the house.

It was a whole new world outside—a world to gasp at even as you stumbled and slid and ran over the slippery cobblestones of the street. It was a whole new world—still and stunned, cold and white. A thin white film of snow had come in the night and had dusted everything just enough to make a whole new world of whiteness.

Far down the street, out of sight of the house, Moonta stopped and looked back at the way he had come. He was the first one to have come down the street, the only one anywhere. His track disturbed the street—and that was all. It was as if he were in the new white world alone—he and God. He down here, standing quiet, scared; God up there above the cold, still whiteness he had made. "Snow," Moonta said softly to himself and God. "Snow. Now there's got to be ice." But it was a prayer. "Oh, there must be skating ice on the crisscross network of ditches in the Skate School Field.

But would the ice be safe in just one night? Moonta thought of that after he'd already passed his grandfather's house. It was the last house in the village; beyond it was the Children's Skate School Field, and the ditches.

The snow that had dusted everything with a film would make it hard to see if the ice was safe. Ice, Moonta knew, did not freeze equally thick everywhere along a ditch. There might be spots of thin, weak ice, but the snow would hide it. Why, if you went through the ice in this cold, you'd freeze solid. He stood, doubtful, then turned and ran back to Grandpa's barn. If he had Grandpa's barn broom, he could sweep the ice out ahead of him as he skated down the ditches. Then he'd surely see if it wasn't safe in spots.

He doubled back in the stillness. Nothing moved—no one was outside. Only here and there did a thick plume of black smoke rising straight up out of a chimney show that inside the houses people were getting up and stoking their stoves. There wasn't even a dog outside. Only a cat track marched across the street straight toward Grandfather's barn. Moonta jerked the screaking barn door open just enough to squeeze into the barn.

Fortunately the barn broom stood just inside the door. As he grabbed it something squirmed and eeled between his feet. It gave him a horrible scare, but it was only the cat. Now he and the cat made new tracks going down the street.

But the cat must have thought he was chasing it, because with wild miaows and big jumps it made for a little house where the smoke was pluming. Moonta dashed past the house with his broom before they could open the door and see him.

There was ice! Why, the very first ditch of the Skate School Field alongside the road looked frozen solid. And no wonder, for it was so cold that by this time his hands were already numb around the thick broom handle. Even his cheeks were stiff with cold. Strangely, the tip of his nose hurt, but not his ears. He pulled his stocking cap down far over his ears and pulled up the woolen muffler around his neck so it covered his mouth and nose. He pulled down his sweater sleeves until they all but covered his fingertips.

With numb, clumsy hands he reversed the broom and let the end of the thick, heavy handle crash down on the ice. The broom handle went straight through. It made a neat, round hole.

In utter disappointment Moonta stumbled up and ran into the field to another ditch. Again he let the broom handle crash. This time it bounced up, it didn't go through. Moonta almost cried. This was ice, safe skating ice. He didn't wait; he opened his sweater and pulled out his skates. But as he did so he saw a thick, round boulder lying gray in the rimy, white frozen grass.

Moonta had to kick the boulder loose, it was frozen to the

ground. The boulder was so viciously cold to his numbed fingers, it made him a little sick to his stomach, but he carried it over to the ditch. The boulder hit the ice with a cracking, booming sound that traveled far down the ditch. But it didn't go through, it bounced up and skittered across the ice to the opposite bank. This was ice. This was safe.

Moonta blew on his fingers to limber them enough so he could tie his skates to his shoes. But he found that the leather thongs of his skates were so stiff from the cold, they wouldn't knot. He chewed the ends of the thongs, then fast as he could, clumsily, hastily, any old way, he tied the skates to his feet.

Moonta let himself down in the ditch almost the way he let himself out of bed. Only this time he had to hang on with both hands to the cold, bare branch of a snowy bush. Then he stood on ice—on his skates!

He looked up and down the ditch. He grabbed the broom, made one sweeping motion with it, and started to skate away. The very same moment both his feet skittered crazily from under him. He threw himself forward, but his feet shot out from under him backward; he desperately threw himself backward, wildly windmilling his arms. It made no difference what he did, his feet went any crazy way they wanted. In his wild lurchings he got the broom between his legs. It tripped him, he pitched forward over the broom, fell hard, shot across the ice, and rammed face up against the opposite bank. The fall knocked the wind out of him, knocked his mouth open—

58

his open mouth buried itself in the icy grass of the bank. He spat and blew, felt pieces of cold dirt and frozen grass between his teeth. He pulled himself up by the icy grass, tearing out handfuls, but his skates wouldn't stay under him. The moment he stood erect and free from the bank, he fell back hard. He crashed to the ice the way a tree falls. He could hear his head clunk against the ice.

Stunned, he sat up slowly, gingerly. He felt the back of his head. Then he sat flat on the ice, legs sprawled wide apart, and cried. Oh, he wasn't crying, he told himself, because he'd hit his head; he was crying because he couldn't skate. He couldn't skate a stroke—not even one simple, single stroke.

Somehow in all the winters when he'd thought and dreamed of skating, he'd always just pictured himself skating away, easy and winging, the way a bird flies. Oh, he'd known he still had to learn to skate, but he'd wanted it so hard all these years and he'd thought about it so much, it seemed as if he'd only have to get on skates. He groaned in angry disappointment. He couldn't even stand on skates!

Bitter big tears crawled over his cold, stiff cheeks.

A voice above him said, "Blubbering on a cold morning like this isn't going to make you a bit warm. Imagine having to go to school pretty soon with frozen tears stuck to your cheeks . . . although maybe I can chisel them off with my jackknife."

It was Grandfather. Moonta didn't have to look up to know that, and he didn't. He swallowed his crying, but he sat where he was, spraddle-legged on the ice. Grandpa must be standing there on the ditch bank looking down at him. Moonta didn't want to get up, or look up.

"I can't skate," he sniveled up at last in the silence. "I

can't skate a stroke. Grandpa, I can't even stand on skates!"

"Here, get up," Grandpa ordered. "And crawl over and hand up that broom."

"I took it out of your barn without asking," Moonta admitted miserably.

"Yes, I know." Grandfather grinned. "It's a poor morning for crime and thievery. All I had to do was to follow your tracks—and there you sat. And there you still sit."

"But I can't skate, Grandpa," he insisted desperately. He didn't care anything about the miserable broom.

"Neither can anybody else—until he learns," Grandpa said. "Did you think you were different?"

"No, but I'm so old. . . . "

"That you are," Grandfather somberly agreed. "Older than the sea, almost. But look, I'm nine times older than you are and all my life I've wanted to fly, but I can't fly. So what's being old have to do with it?"

"If you came down here and held me up, maybe I could skate," Moonta suggested in a small voice. "I can't stay up."

"Wouldn't dare," Grandpa said quietly. "I'm not only nine times as old, but I'm six times as heavy as you are, and that ice that is sort of holding you up might not hold us both. It's asking a bit too much from one night of ice. But here, grab the handle of the broom. . . . "

That is the way they did it. Grandfather held the bristle

61

end of the broom and walked along the ditch bank; Moonta, down below, clutched the handle in a death grip, and Grandpa pulled him along.

But not for long. "Hey," Grandpa ordered. "You can't use your skates as runners—you're not learning to be a sled. Move those feet."

Hesitantly, timidly, almost climbing up the broom handle with his hands, Moonta tried small, scratchy strokes. It worked. It worked! He was skating!

"Where are your mittens?" Grandpa suddenly asked. "You, with bare, blue hands in this cold . . . Moonta, did you sneak out of the house without your folks knowing?"

Just as Grandpa was saying that, a voice answered across the field, "Yes, he did, that's exactly what he did. And you, aiding and abetting him in your old age." It was Father.

"I didn't know," Grandpa said over his shoulder to Father. "You come on up out of there," he ordered Moonta. Unceremoniously Grandfather dragged him up the bank, while he clutched the broom handle. Now Father stood there beside Grandpa, looking at Moonta coming up.

"Easy now," he heard Grandfather say softly out of the side of his mouth to Father. "If you'd had to wait four winters for ice, you'd be doing desperate things too."

Father's face didn't change a bit, and now Moonta stood before him. "Off with those skates," Father said.

Moonta bent down to obey, but he couldn't untie the

leather thongs. His hands were too stiff, his fingers were like wood. While Grandfather chafed and chafed Moonta's icy hands, Father hunched down and took off the skates.

Father was so much the skater, he forgot for a moment that he was angry, and said to Moonta, "Next time you tie skates under your shoes get them over closer to the inner edge of the shoe. You don't place them dead center."

Grandfather, still rubbing and rubbing Moonta's hands, agreed with Father. "Yes, I noticed it when I was pulling him. He thought he was skating, but he was really skating on the edges of his shoe soles. Not weak ankles, I hope?"

"No!" Father wouldn't hear of it. "No—just bad tying."

"Well, you never know," Grandfather said, nettled. "Look at his Aunt Cora. Poor Cora could never skate a stroke because of her ankles—and Moonta's mother a champion."

Father had the skates off. "Now run," he ordered, "and run faster than you ran here after you sneaked out of the house. Show your mother you're alive. She's sure you're at the bottom of the canal."

Moonta ran, but he turned to ask, "Is there ice on the canal?"

"Yes," Father said. "But that has nothing to do with you— you're running straight home. And I don't know after this if we'll let you skate again—even if there's ice all winter. Your mother's worried sick."

"I haven't got weak ankles?"

63

"No. No."

"Honest, Grandpa?"

"No, it was just bad tying," Grandpa assured him. "Now run."

He ran gladly, willingly then—fast as he could. He was bubbling inside, no matter how cold he was, no matter how disappointed that he hadn't learned quickly to skate all by himself before anybody was up. He burst through the front door and yelled down the long hall, "Mother! Mother, where are you? Mother, I can skate—a little bit."

He couldn't really skate, he thought, as he tugged the lower and upper doors shut, but he'd learn as fast as he could. Then he'd be ready to skate on the canal with the whole village when the ice got thick enough. There wouldn't be a soul left in the village, except babies and Aunt Cora. . . . He'd never known that as big as she was, Aunt Cora had weak ankles. It was a sorry thing.

He ran down the hall. "Mother," he yelled again. "Mother, there's ice on the canal—Father said so. . . . "

The kitchen door opened. It was Mother. "Yes, and I saw so," she said. "I was out to that canal twice—scared! I'm still shaking."

There Mother stood at the far end of the hall. She filled the doorway, hands in her sides, arms akimbo, face strict and stern. It made the walk down the hall the longest walk that could be walked. Moonta's feet dragged.

64

"I think I froze my hands," he said pitifully.

"I think you froze your head," Mother said, unrelenting. "You certainly didn't use a single brain cell in it. Oh, that was sneaky, Moonta. I didn't know you were sneaky."

At that moment, in the warmth of the house his hands began to pain. They must be frozen. He walked slowly toward Mother. Then he remembered that Father had kept his skates. This time, he was sure, Father would hide them where he would never find them. And Mother would never let him go out to the Children's Skate School Field again.

"I froze my hands," he said again, so he could start to cry—as if about that.

5

All Ten Fingers

ALL OF a sudden Moonta really, honestly howled out because of his hands. He screamed. He turned away from Mother and ran down the hall into the living room, stopping only to buckle over and squeeze his hands between his legs. He moaned with the pain, shook his hands—blew on them, wrung them—anything. . . . Never had he known such sudden, terrible, fierce pain. Ten-times-over pain in all his ten fingers.

Mother, who had been going to be stern, was scared, but he wasn't putting on—not even one tiny bit. The warmth in the house had hit his wooden, numbed hands, until it was as

66

if his fingers screamed out with pain. He ran desperately back and forth, bent double over his hands, squeezing his fingers.

Mother ran after him into the living room, but he squirmed away from her, ran into the kitchen. She ran out into the yard and tried to scrape the snow dust together with her bare hands, but there wasn't enough, and she came running back into the kitchen. She kept asking, "Where's your father? Where's your father?"

"I left him with Grandpa," Moonta gasped out. Then, because of the pain, he had to run again. He ran from the kitchen to the living room, from the living room to the kitchen, up and down the hall, always doubled over, clenching and wringing his fingers.

Mother finally caught him by the shoulders and steered him to the kitchen sink. Then, because she didn't know what else to do, she plunged his hands into a basin of water. The first plunge was awful. It was almost as if the pain tore at the top of his head and lifted it. But gradually the pain began to lessen.

He pulled his hands out and smiled a weak smile up at Mother, and right then he wet his pants just a little, just from the sudden relief. Why, his hands felt like hands again—soft and painless. It was a sweet, weak wonder. Again he smiled a shamed smile at Mother, because, well, he'd wet his pants —just a little.

"It's better. I'm better. It's over," he whispered.

Tears came to Mother's eyes. She sat down at the table and in one long *slurp* gulped down a whole cup of cold coffee. "Moonta, Moonta," she whispered. "Sometimes I wish I had ten children because one's too much trouble. But often I wish I had none. . . . And I don't mean *that* for one silly, darn moment." Then Mother leaned over and hauled him to her, and kissed the top of his head.

Oh, he loved her, and his hands didn't hurt, and softly he asked, "After school can I go skating again on the ditches?"

"Of course you may," Mother answered. "But I'm going to make you wear two pairs of mittens. Why, I'll mitten you to death the rest of this winter, lest I die from sheer scare myself." Big as he was, and in the fourth grade, she hauled him into her lap and pulled off his pants and his underwear. "I'll get you dry ones," she said. "You can't go to school like that." But she didn't say anything more.

It was shameful just the same, so he asked quickly, "May I have my breakfast now?"

"Boys," Mother said. "Men! I'll never understand them— not in two hundred years. Worlds of agony one moment, the next moment hunger and breakfast."

She slid Moonta off her lap. "Come get dressed while I make breakfast for you and your father. I'll be lucky if I can eat by noon."

When Moonta came back to the kitchen, Mother asked, "Now where's your father staying? I wouldn't put it past him —if he can get those skates of yours on his feet—that he went skating on one of those ditches himself."

That was how it turned out. As if he had heard Mother's words, at that moment Father opened the kitchen door. Moonta saw them at once—the points of his skates sticking out of Father's pants pockets. The first thing when Father came in he said, "I couldn't resist—just had to try it a minute. Of course with Moonta's little skates, I had to tie them to my socks." He held up one foot. "Guess these socks are a mess."

69

Then he sniffed. "Boy, breakfast! Skating sure is hungry work."

"Yes, I know," Mother said. But strangely, at the stove, frying the bacon, she stood crying a little. She turned her head away from Moonta, but she seemed to be sputtering to herself among the sputtering sounds of bacon. Then Moonta heard her say: "Why is it that men can stay babies, but women can't?" Then she turned to Father and asked, "Four slices of bacon this morning?"

Father said, "No, make it six."

Right after Father, Moonta said, "Me too."

Mother gave him a look. "Go change your socks," she told Father.

Moonta stood waiting for Father to come back, wishing he hadn't asked for those six slices of bacon. Why hadn't he thought of it before? If after the awful pain in his hands he'd acted sick and had asked to go back to bed, maybe he wouldn't have to go to school. No, it wouldn't work. If he went to bed it would be bed the rest of the day. With Mother it was bed or school, and bed was worse than school any day. It was a shame. It would have been a fine chance to practice skating, with all the other kids in school—but there was no way to make it work. He sighed and asked, "May I have six slices too, Mother?"

Mother looked at him and said: "Big man!"

Moonta blushed. Father came back into the kitchen, but

70

Mother didn't tell him a thing, not even about the almost frozen fingers.

The day at school was an eternity—the longest day that had ever been. The minutes on the clock that hung at the front of the room simply would not tick themselves off. The minute hand seemed like the hour hand. The sheet-metal stove roared and rattled with the big fire inside, but the heat didn't melt the frost on the flowered windows. A grave, still light came through the thick windows. It was the only cheering thing in the whole room. It meant that outside it was still freezing as hard as ever.

No matter what the subject was, or what the headmaster said as he moved from one class to the other in the big room all the afternoon, Moonta couldn't fix his mind on anything but the dead clock. In the middle of the afternoon, from the other classroom behind the folding doors just back of Moonta's seat, there came a loud cheering and an excited babble of talk. It went on so long the headmaster had to stop in the instructions he was giving to the fifth grade. He turned to the whole room and said, "I would guess from the noise and excitement, the master of the first three grades has just told his pupils that school, for them, will be out in a few minutes, in order that they can go out and learn to skate in the Children's Skate School Field."

Right in front of Moonta on the fourth grade side of the

71

room, the fat girl, Knilliska, shot her hand into the air. Then she blurted out, "Master, is it true that there's skating ice on the canal now?"

The headmaster stood silent at the front of the room until the whole room had gone deadly silent. First Knilliska's neck went red, then it went white. All eyes in the room turned on her.

Now at last the headmaster said sternly and slowly, "Knilliska, we were talking about the little people in the other room, so your question seems most appropriate." He made an awful pause. Only the clock ticked. Then he said: "For a first grader!"

Softly Knilliska began to shake and cry.

"Yes," the headmaster went on. "Yes, the state of the ice on the canal might be of some importance, but of course not of the first importance to us who are scholars and students. The state of the canal, Knilliska, will become important to you when you run out there the moment that school is out— along with, I'd guess, every other pupil in this room." The headmaster made a pause again, this time for a joke. "And, students, I promise I won't be very far behind on my old legs. The only reason I'll be behind is because I'll have stopped off at my house next door to pick up my skates— just on the faint chance that there'll be safe ice on the canal."

The whole room laughed excitedly, and was almost as noisy as the small room had been. But Knilliska's shoulders still shook as she cried silently.

The headmaster raised his eyebrows, the whole room became still, the clock ticked again. Solemnly the master went on: "Since we are now on the subject of ice and skating, I have been asked that all you upper-class pupils will stay off the ditches of the Children's Skate School Field. Knilliska" —the master interrupted himself—"if you can't stop crying, why don't you stand at the front of the room under the clock. Quite often when we can't control ourselves, just knowing that others are watching us helps our poor self-control."

Knilliska erupted from her seat, flung herself, sobbing, to the front of the room, and pressed her forehead to the blackboard under the clock.

Everything waited until Knilliska took her place. Now the headmaster went on as if nothing had happened. "The reason we ask this—as you well know—is because for the past winters there has been no ice, so the little children had no chance to learn. Are there any questions?"

At the back of the room Moonta started to raise his hand. Then the big, empty space right in front of him, caused by Knilliska's having to stand under the clock, stopped him cold. The headmaster turned to him and said, "Yes, Moonta, did you have a question?"

Moonta dumbly shook his head. He might have been able to ask his question from behind Knilliska's back, but with the empty space before him, he couldn't admit to the whole room that he, a fourth grader, couldn't skate.

He shuddered at the thought. He was still nervous in the

big room with all the big fifth and sixth graders. He'd only passed into the big room the first of the year—about ten days ago. The headmaster still awed him.

He had wanted to ask, "But what about me? Can't I go there? Because I don't know how to skate. I was sick that last winter of ice."

In his mind he changed the "can't" to "mayn't," but he still could not ask the question out loud. Everybody would turn to look at him, and the master might make a joke about it in his slow, solemn voice.

Moonta's mind had been so busy, the headmaster's voice startled him. "We're waiting, Moonta," he said. "Fifty-six of us are waiting for your one small question."

"Oh, I'm sorry, Master. I meant to say No . . . no, sir, I have no question."

"Thank you, Moonta." The headmaster bowed his head until all his gray hair showed. "For a moment there you looked so crestfallen we were a bit worried you might burst out in tears like Knilliska, and that would have been quite a duet from seat to seat."

The whole room laughed and laughed. Moonta sat still-faced, looking straight ahead of him at the clock above Knilliska. His cheeks felt almost as stiff as they had felt this morning when they were stiff with cold, but now they were hot and red.

At last the eyes turned away from him, and the headmaster

said: "So it is understood, then—not one of us will skate on the children's ditches. Like the grown-ups, you will wait until ice comes to the canal. Of course we have no real control over you once you leave this school. But . . . if we hear of any of you skating there, let me remind you that there is school again tomorrow . . . and that we will be most unhappy with you when you get back to school. Well, then, fifth grade, shall we return to reciting geography? And all the other grades back to your studies—and, Knilliska, back to your seat."

The blow had fallen. He mightn't skate in the Skate School Field. Moonta felt as if he had been hit on the head. He sat mute and stunned as the day wore on. It was more awful now, for behind the folding doors there was absolute silence. While the big room had been laughing about him, the little kids in the other room must have been let out of school so they could learn to skate. Right now they were all learning to skate on the ditches of the Skate Field, but he mightn't even go there.

At last school was out. Everybody tore out of the room. In the hall they ran to their numbered cubicles, ripped their wooden shoes out, shot their feet into them; swung coats, sweaters, and mufflers around them; and stormed out of school. The whole school, everybody, was going to the canal. Knilliska was in the midst of them all. She was red in the face

from blushing. She was a heroine now. Everybody—even the boys—slapped her on the back. Once far enough away from school, they all began yelling things like, "Good for you, Knilliska. Good for you. Wish I'd done it. Wish I'd asked it. Oh, man, you sure got us out of a lot of work. It really got him talking. . . . "

Everybody was running out ahead of Moonta. He dribbled on behind because he had nowhere to go, nothing to do.

Because of the headmaster he couldn't even go to learn on the ditches of the Skate Field. He couldn't do anything— nothing at all. Now he'd never learn to skate.

Moonta walked on alone. Everybody had run out of sight. But if there was skating ice on the canal, they'd all come running back to get their skates. The little kids were skating on the ditches. Everybody would be skating. But he—he had nothing to do; nothing.

6

The Skate School Field

MOTHER was home. "I'm just back from the canal," she told Moonta as he came into the kitchen. "Have you been there?"

"No," Moonta said. "I can't skate."

"Well, I know that," Mother said impatiently, "but you can look."

"And I mayn't skate on the ditches of the Skate School Field."

"Who says so?" Mother demanded.

"The headmaster says so."

"Oh," Mother said in a smaller voice. She listened patiently while Moonta explained.

"But didn't you tell him that your case was different because you'd been sick? And that even though you are in the fourth grade . . ."

Moonta made a noise. Mother always seemed to think it was the easiest thing to tell a teacher anything you wanted to tell him. "They'd all have laughed," Moonta told her.

"You could have gone up to him afterward," Mother said. Then she got angry. "Anyway, it isn't his field. What must have happened is that some of the young mothers asked him to announce it. That doesn't mean it's a law. You've just as much right to learn as any of the five-year-olds. . . . Come on—and I'd like to see anybody stop me, even a headmaster." Mother looked around, grabbed her scarf, and started to knot it around her head.

"Are you going along?" Moonta quavered. Now it was much worse—all the big kids at the canal, and his mother taking him by the hand to the Skate Field—like a four-year-old.

Mother knotted the scarf under her chin with still another angry knot. "But I thought you wanted me to! I thought you were desperate to learn to skate— Oh, yes," she said to herself more softly, "I guess I understand. . . . Well, you go ahead, and you skate on any of those ditches. Yours is a special case, and you've got just as much right. Oh, your skates are up on the shelf in the turf bin where your father stuck them this morning."

Moonta was glad to go to the turf bin. He sighed to himself. He wished Father was home. Father would know much better what rights he had than Mother. Mother always had to get angry before she talked about rights. She never sounded too sure.

From the kitchen Mother called, "I'm going to the store, but I've laid an extra pair of mittens on the table here. Stick them in your pocket, so when your other ones get wet . . . Maybe I'll come along later and see how you're doing. That is, if you'll let me."

"Oh, sure, Mother," Moonta yelled out heartily, but he waited in the turf bin until she had left. He had a wonderful thought. If there was ice, the ground was frozen too, so Grandfather wouldn't have gone to his little piece of land outside the village. He'd stop on his way to the Skate Field and ask Grandpa: Did he, or did he not, have a right to skate on the ditches? He shoved his skates in his pockets exactly the way his father had had them in his pockets this morning and started off.

Grandfather wasn't home. The house door was locked. Moonta pulled out the bottom of the hasped barn door and squeezed through. He waited for Grandfather, but it was cold and dark in the barn. There was no sound of footsteps coming near, but even inside, Moonta could hear the excited

79

bee-buzz of voices from the Skate Field. It was so still that sometimes he could hear shouts coming from the canal clear across the village.

Mother had said that he had just as much right as anyone else. She'd said the Skate School Field belonged to the village. It didn't belong to the parson or the headmaster, even if they were the most important people in the village. It belonged to everyone.

Moonta eased himself out of the barn, but the door pinched and squeezed, and one of the skates in his pocket got caught crosswise. The sharp heel of the skate dug into his leg. Outside the barn he took his extra mittens and pulled one over the end of each skate. Now no one would know, and if the headmaster was at the field, Moonta decided he would just stand and look. There was no law against that.

The near ditches closest to the road were crowded with little children and their mothers. Every little kid was learning to skate. It was amazing how many. You wouldn't think there were that many in the whole village. Many of the mothers just walked along the banks of the ditches, but others were down on the ice, holding up their children. Some of the smallest children pushed little chairs ahead of themselves as they scrabbled and scratched on their skates down the crowded ditches. It was a mixed-up, noisy excitement.

Moonta stood and watched it a long while. Then, since nobody paid any attention to him and the headmaster wasn't there, he lowered himself down the ditch bank and stood and watched some more. Now the little children scrabbled all around him. Their mothers picked them up when they fell, and wiped their noses when they cried. One mother near Moonta was warming her little boy's hands by breathing hard on them. She looked up at Moonta—her name was Af, he remembered.

"Well, Moonta, you can't skate with your skates in your pocket," Af said. "Better get busy skating, or pretty soon you'll be bawling from the cold, and I'll have to hot-breathe you back to life."

Moonta laughed and laughed. Af was nice. She was friendly. He tugged his skates out of his pockets—Af had seen what they were anyway, even with the mittens on them —and kneeled in the ditch to put them on. He worked hard at it, trying to remember exactly how Father had said to do it, so he wouldn't tip over on his ankles and skate on the edge of his shoe soles.

Then, as he kneeled, two little girl skaters ran into him and knocked him full length on the ice. On top of the bank a young woman saw him sprawled and thought he had fallen. She laughed at him. "If you haven't learned how to skate yet, Moonta, fellow," she said "it isn't much use anymore is it? What's the matter—weak ankles?"

"I got knocked down," Moonta said. "I was trying my skates."

81

"Oh?" she said. "But aren't you a bit big for these little kid ditches—you looked so long all sprawled out."

Just then her own little girl fell in a tumble and jumble of little kids and got her hand scratched. The woman slid down the bank and ran to her screaming child. She hadn't given Moonta time to explain that he'd been sick that last winter of ice. With the woman busy, Moonta hurriedly finished knotting the second skate under his shoe. He wanted to get away before the sharp-voiced woman came back with more to say. She'd acted as if it were her ditch, when it didn't even belong to the burgomaster of the whole county. . . . Moonta looked along the ditch. Mother hadn't come yet.

Now Moonta rose up as if to skate away. He actually managed a few wild strokes, but he had to thresh about and windmill his arms so wildly, he knocked down a little boy that got in his way. Moonta lost all control. He whipped about in a crazy, staggering half circle, then fell on the boy he had knocked down.

Before Moonta could get up, so many children crashed into him, the way he lay sprawled crossways over the narrow ditch, that in no time he lay, face mashed against the ice, under a pile of little kids. Mothers came running and yelling, sliding down the bank to unscramble the pile. Indignant women on top of the bank shouted directions and instructions to them. At last Moonta could sit up. The little boy skater sat up, bewildered, next to him.

"Oh, you're heavy," he said to Moonta.

Some of the women around them laughed, but others looked at Moonta with hard, angry eyes.

"Just what is that big lunker doing down here?" one woman asked. "What's he doing on a beginners' ditch?"

A woman standing near Moonta pulled him up. "Look," she called up to the women on the bank. "Almost as big as I am."

"Can't you wait, like the rest of us?" a big girl yelled out. She was standing with the mothers, but Moonta recognized her—she was Klaska. She was in the sixth grade. "Wait until the headmaster finds out about you!" she threatened.

Suddenly Moonta was angry, so angry he would have stamped his foot if he had dared. He yelled back at Klaska, "I have to learn, too, don't I? I was sick that whole week the last winter we had ice, so I still have to learn, don't I?"

"Sick, eh?" a hard-faced woman said. "Sick in bed, or sick in the ankles? Anyway, that was your hard luck, wasn't it? Just because you were sick doesn't mean that a big kid like you can windmill around on these ditches and knock all the little kids black and blue."

Moonta's mouth fell open as he looked up at her. "But they fell on *me*," he said. He choked on the words. She didn't care. None of them cared that he'd been sick and still had to learn. All they cared about was their own children. If only Mother were here. He felt alone and scared, and angry and outraged

83

at the same time. He blazed with indignation. He screeched out at all of them, "It isn't your ditch. It's everybody's ditch. So there!"

But the women on top of the ditch had all turned around; they were looking down the road toward the village. Now their voices were soft and nice. Moonta heard one of them say, "Imagine them both coming to see how our little ones are doing—both the minister and the headmaster. That shows interest."

They all were turned around—their bodies even leaned forward a little—and they were murmuring among themselves. It almost sounded like cooing.

Only the big girl, Klaska, turned to look at Moonta.

"Is it really the headmaster?" he asked urgently.

First Klaska looked as if she weren't going to answer, but then she got a little red in the face and nodded. "The preacher, too," she half whispered. "And it looks like the whole big room from school is with them. . . . Why even the young fellows of the village are coming—it must be they can't work in the fields."

She straightened herself and felt her hair. The women were all babbling. Even the little kids in the ditch around Moonta had stopped and stood looking up. Out of nothing but desperation Moonta whirled, struck out down the ditch, and skated away. He hurtled, fell forward, and stumbled more than he skated, but he didn't go down. It was more a running

84

on skates than it was skating, but somehow he twisted in among the little kids, somehow got around them without knocking them down. He scrambled on wildly. At last there was a crossditch. Moonta threw one scared look back as he whipped around the corner into the crossditch.

In that wild glance Moonta saw the headmaster. He was standing with the minister, talking to the group of women. It didn't look as if the headmaster had seen him.

Because of the half look over his shoulder, Moonta couldn't straighten out after he whirled into the new ditch. He smashed hard against the frozen bank. For a moment he rested there, gasping his relief that he was out of sight.

The next moment he straightened out. He was too close to the roadside ditch. The women would tell the headmaster; Klaska was sure to tell. And everybody from the big room was there—how they'd laugh if the headmaster caught him.

Fear made Moonta skate again. Fear seemed to keep him on his feet for as many as twenty, thirty scratchy strokes. Then he'd smash to the ice again; but he'd pick himself up, lunge ahead. He had to get away from the roadside ditch— any old way—no matter how much he fell, no matter how it hurt.

He came to another ditch and blindly plunged into it. This was a wider, deeper ditch with high banks. Nobody could see him now. Not even the top of his stocking cap would show. Now for the first time he felt safe. There was no one here anywhere. Moonta felt safe enough to stop to take his stocking cap off and roll it up. He got down on one knee so his skates wouldn't skitter from under him, and rolled the cap into a tight, hard roll. There, now even if it did leave his ears out in the cold, it wouldn't hurt so much when the back of his head clunked against the ice. That was the worst— falling backward. But now the back of his head would be cushioned.

Moonta got up, stumbled on again, but couldn't seem to get going properly. He stopped, looked down to see if his feet were set right to make the first stroke, then he looked back. To his horror he saw that in the place where he had been kneeling the ice had bowed down like a bowl.

Moonta knew then that he had blundered on to a draught ditch. He sucked in his breath—this was one of the central, main ditches that drained the water from the whole field of ditches and sent it on its way to the canal. It had a current, and because of the current the ice was thin. Here it was too thin to hold him in one spot. Where he had kneeled it had been tough enough just to bend and bow and not break, but he mustn't stand anyplace in this ditch. Moonta desperately looked up at the banks, but they were so straight and freshly dug, there was nothing to grab onto to pull himself up.

He looked behind him again. Now there was a little water standing in the cupped bowl that his knee had made. He couldn't go back that way. Way up ahead there seemed to

86

be a break in the ditch wall—that must be a crossditch. There was nothing for it but to try to make it. Desperately he reminded himself he mustn't run on his skates—that pounded. He mustn't fall or crash to the ice—it might break. Somehow he had to move smoothly—skate and glide, not run or scramble. Oh, it was quiet and still. He was all alone. Draught ditches were deep; it would be awful to go down all alone. . . . Carefully, cautiously, Moonta tried to move ahead on his skates. He had to get to that crossditch.

As he moved along, heart clammily in his throat, eyes fixed on the ice ahead, to his gasping relief Moonta suddenly wasn't alone. He heard loud voices coming over the field. Then he heard the clatter of many wooden shoes over the frozen ground. Moonta couldn't see anything from the deep ditch, but the loud voices and the clatter of the shoes seemed to be coming straight toward him. Then he realized what it was, and the gasp of relief died. It was the "Over The Paper Ceiling" game. The young men of the village were playing "Over The Paper Ceiling." They did it every year.

Moonta skated frantically to get out of their way.

"Over The Paper Ceiling" was a rough, dangerous game— a dare game. A whole row of young fellows, arms tightly around one another's waist, would run across the fields on their wooden shoes, plunge down into the ditches, and run full speed over the ice to the opposite bank. It all had to be done before the ice could break and give way under their weight. Anyone that let go was an utter coward and a sissy. Anybody that went through the ice and had to be hauled out of the water was a "pickerel." There was even a song they chanted about it.

The rest of the fellows would take him up on their shoulders, put their coats over him, and carry him all through the village and sing out for everybody to hear:

> *A pickerel, a pickerel,*
> *We've got us a pickerel,*
> *A wet, sick, limp pickerel,*
> *Down deep in this bag.*

All the kids of the village would follow on behind. Everybody would laugh and poke fun at the wet, miserable, cold fellow. But his own buddies wouldn't let him go until he'd been carried down the whole length of Main Street. After that they'd plunk him down in front of his own house with a kick in the pants from all of them for being so clumsy and being a "pickerel."

Moonta still scampered to get out ahead of the coming gang of young fellows. He somehow kept his feet under him, somehow skated, but always it sounded as if they were coming straight at him. Now there was a change of sound as the row of young men must have plunged down into a ditch and scrambled up the other bank without the ice giving way.

"Aw, this is no fun," one of them yelled out. "This ice is too strong. Hey, let's try the main draught ditch."

There was laughing and kidding and joshing—the row must have lined up again. Then came the hard clatter of their wooden shoes over the frozen ground. Wild as he skated and raced, it still sounded to Moonta as if always they were coming straight at him. He couldn't seem to get away from them. He whimpered a little as he clawed to get to the nearest crossditch.

Now there were no voices. Now there was only the sharp clatter of the wooden shoes. They must all be saving their breath for the plunge into the draught ditch, and the extra bit of nerve and muscle it would take to scramble up the far bank.

Suddenly their dark figures loomed up above the high ditch bank. Moonta lunged away from them. Behind him there was a combined letting out of breath, and then a rough gasping as the whole row plunged across the ditch. Somehow they must have made it over the thin ice by sheer speed. Behind Moonta there was an excited gabble as they congratulated each other. "Boy," one of them yelled. "Boy, that was close. That was a near one. Hey, fellows, look! No ice. The ice caved to the bottom. Anybody get wet—anybody?"

Moonta threw one frightened look over his shoulder. There was black water behind him—it was coming on. The ice that had gone down under the young men was sending a wave of black water around Moonta. Water came curling, licking around his skates. Then it raced ahead of him.

Moonta tried to scramble ahead, but the black water reaching out for him made him lose all control. With a wild scream he fell headlong, and the water spattered over him. He fell on ice, but he lay in water. He couldn't get his feet under him, his skates skittered sideways and wouldn't take hold on the watery ice.

"Help!" Moonta screamed.

Behind him there were startled shouts. "Look, a kid. We knocked the ice out from behind him. Come on—get that kid."

There was a clattering run of wooden shoes. "Watch it," one of them shouted. "If we slide down in there, we'll cave the ice from under him. Watch it. . . . "

Moonta crawled on like a drowning rat. The water crawled with him, and out ahead of him. It was ugly and numbingly cold. It licked at him, raced ahead, and curled back long black fingers out for him.

"Here, hold hands," a voice ordered. "I'll slide down and grab him, and you pull us up. Stop crawling, kid . . . I'll get you."

The one who had been let down the bank of the ditch grabbed, missed, then got Moonta by the sweater collar. He was hauled up like a drowned puppy. His sweater came up around his face, his sleeves cut into his arms, but up he came.

90

When they jerked his sweater down, Moonta was in a ring of young men, all looking at him with hard, excited eyes—as if it were his fault. "What'd you think you were doing skating on a draught ditch all alone? How could we know there'd be a darn fool skating on a draught ditch after only one night of ice? And stop your blubbering; you're not drowned!"

"I'm not blubbering—it's my teeth," Moonta managed to say. His teeth were chattering so hard he could hardly talk.

"Who are you?" one of them asked.

For a second Moonta was indignant that they didn't know him, but then he didn't know them either—they were too old. "Moonta," he said, "Moonta of the carpenter."

"Oh, sure, that's right," somebody said. "Hey, Leendert, he's the son of your new boss."

"All right, then," Leendert said, taking over. "Let's get those wet clothes off him, or he'll be the dead son of my boss."

He stripped Moonta's sweater over his head, not bothering about the buttons. He looked doubtful for a moment, took off Moonta's skates and shoes, and then his pants too. Two of the young men gave up their jackets. The jackets were miles too big; they covered Moonta completely, but they were warm from the young men's bodies—they felt good. Shivering and shaking, Moonta snuggled himself inside of them.

91

Leendert, without a further word, slung Moonta over his shoulder as if he were a bag of old clothes and started away on a trot. He led the way, but all the others came on behind in a long file. Then the jogging and jiggling worked the jackets up around Moonta's head, and he couldn't see anymore. ·

"Golly," Leendert said softly to Moonta, "and just last week I started to work for your father. But how could we know there'd be anybody on that draught ditch? We were just killing time and having some fun till there'd be skating on the canal. Can't lay brick this kind of weather."

"Oh," Moonta said, muffled, through the jacket. "Then you're Leendert. My father has been talking about you. He says you're going to make a good carpenter and bricklayer."

"Did he say that?" Leendert sounded pleased. "Well, let's get you home before you freeze solid or catch pneumonia and I lose my job."

They jogged slantwise across the fields. Leendert even jumped the crossditches with Moonta on his shoulder. The jackets were pulled so far over Moonta's head that he couldn't see anything. "Leendert," he begged, "not toward the beginners' ditches, please. The headmaster's there, and if he finds out I was skating . . . "

"Is he still as mean as ever?" Leendert asked. "All right, but then I'll have to take you around by Main Street."

"I don't care," Moonta said. Anything would be better than having the headmaster see him. Anyway, no one could see who he was, all bundled out of sight in the two big jackets.

One of the fellows behind Moonta and Leendert started the chant the moment they got on Main Street. Then they were all singing:

> *A pickerel, a pickerel,*
> *We've got us a pickerel,*
> *A wet, sick, limp pickerel,*
> *Down deep in this bag.*

"Cut it out, fellows," Leendert begged. "This is the boss's son, and I need that job, I've been out of work so long."

They paid no attention; they kept pestering Leendert by singing it still louder. In no time there were other voices, girls' and boys' voices, chanting along.

Moonta shrank deeper into the collars of the two jackets.

Behind him everybody was having fun chanting the silly song and trying to guess who could be the "pickerel" in the bag. The boys tagging along were making all kinds of funny remarks to make the girls laugh and giggle. None of the young men would tell who was inside the jackets. It added to the fun and the mystery. The group grew and grew, the wooden shoes stamped on the cobblestones in time to the chanted song.

The next moment everything went quiet. Everybody stopped, everything stood still. Leendert stood with Moonta draped across his shoulder.

Out of the silence the minister said in his church-pulpit voice: "Isn't it strange that in this land of water it is so shameful a thing to get a dunking in a ditch, or the canal, or the sea?"

Then, just as Moonta had feared, the headmaster's voice answered: "I've often wondered about it myself. But as you know—we don't learn swimming in this watery land, our summers and our waters are too cold. So my guess would be it got started for no other reason than to scare children away from water and drownings by making a fall into the water utterly ridiculous. You've got to admit, it's the next best thing to learning to swim." Then abruptly the headmaster said, "Well, Leendert, who's the 'pickerel' in the bag this time? And how did it happen?"

As if he were still in school, Leendert politely and obediently explained everything to the headmaster—only he didn't mention Moonta's name. Moonta hung deathly still over Leendert's shoulder, hoping that Leendert wouldn't pull the jackets back so he would have to face the headmaster. That moment the coat collars were peeled back by the headmaster himself. On Leendert's shoulder Moonta's face was on a dead level with the teacher's.

"Moonta!" the master said as if he couldn't believe it. "Didn't I forbid you to skate there—almost the last thing this afternoon? Well, if no pneumonia comes from this, suitable punishment will wait you at school. I promised it. I have to deliver, don't I?"

Moonta nodded miserably.

"Then why did you do it?"

"But I had to learn to skate," Moonta wailed out at the man. "I was sick the last winter we had ice, and now I'm in your room, but I still can't skate."

"That's right," a voice said softly. "I remember now, sir. He was sick that week of ice that year. He was in the first grade in my room then."

Moonta twisted around. It was the young schoolmaster of the three lower grades. Oh, he liked him for saying that. Oh, he wished he was still his teacher.

"You mean," the headmaster said to Moonta, "that you never had a chance to learn, and both your father and mother champions?"

Moonta nodded, his face drained and stiff. He didn't dare to try a single word—he'd blubber.

"Is that what you tried to tell me in class, and then didn't quite dare?" the headmaster persisted.

"They'd all have laughed," Moonta said softly.

"Why would they, if you never had a chance? They once had to learn themselves—one way or another."

Moonta miserably couldn't think of a thing to say.

"Well, Moonta, as poor a skater as I am, I'm too fond of

skating myself not to understand. This changes things. No punishment, boy. And learn hard and fast; then as soon as there's ice on the canal, why, you and I can maybe do a couple of turns together, eh? Just us two duffers."

Moonta's mouth fell open. Tears wanted to come, he was so grateful and so astounded. Why, it was almost as if the headmaster were two people. In school he was stern and made you squirm, but out here on the street he was like any other human being. Why, he'd admitted right out loud in the middle of Main Street that he was a poor skater.

The master must have seen his face working. He reached up and pulled the collars back up around Moonta's head. "Get him home quick," he ordered Leendert. "On the run! And the rest of you—scat. You big fellows, too—endangering a little boy's life with your idiotic games. Grow up. Can't you wait for skating ice? Must you break up what there is with your big, clumsy shoes?"

It was just like in school; they all obeyed. Leendert let Moonta down at the door of his house. He opened the door and called down the hall in a polite voice, "Mrs. Riemersma, your boy's here, and he's a little wet."

Somehow Moonta did not worry too much when Mother came flying down the hall, not even when Leendert handed her his wet clothes. "Mom, Mom," he yelped, impatiently pulling the jackets down from around his mouth, "the headmaster is going skating with me. He promised." It was still the wonder of wonders. "And, Mother, I can skate, when I'm scared enough."

"Scared enough," Mother said hoarsely. "If only you'd ever be scared enough. Now how'd this happen?"

Leendert explained, but he didn't say anything about Moonta's having been on a draught ditch. Leendert hadn't told on him with the headmaster either. He took all the blame. But that was because Father was his boss.

"So you big lunks were playing 'Over the Paper Ceiling,'" Mother said slowly. "You should have had me along, I'd be an expert. That seems to be my whole life with Moonta. I always seem to be going over a paper ceiling. I'm always scared at what he'll do next. . . . But I know now what I'm going to do next," she said to Moonta. "To bed with you!"

She ripped off the two jackets, grabbed Moonta's hand, and ran with him down the hall. "Thanks, Leendert," she called over her shoulder.

Behind them Leendert softly closed the door.

7

Little Red Chair

IT HAD turned out worse than Moonta could have imagined. Mother was really worried about him. Now here he lay in bed, a jug with hot water wrapped in wool against his chest, and another hot crock fitted against his back. It was all to prevent pneumonia from his ice-water soaking in the draught ditch. But Mother had even pushed a hot wrapped-in-wool rock up against his feet. And she'd made him put on itchy wool underwear under his flannel nightgown. Still it was not enough. Now she threw an extra quilt from her own bed on top of all his bedding, and then she made him put on

Grandpa's thick stocking cap instead of his own light sleeping cap. After all that, Mother made him snuggle down under the blankets until only his nose showed.

It was only his nose, Moonta imagined to himself, that acted as a brake to keep him from sliding down under the waves of blankets and drowning in the sweaty, steamy, prickly heat that he himself made in all the woolly warmth.

Mother came back from the kitchen. Now she put a mustard plaster way up between his shoulder blades. She made him push himself up just enough to drink a cup of hot water with some ghastly-tasting medicine in it. It steamed right up under his nose, and if possible, the smell was even worse than the taste. Moonta squirmed and gagged, hoping that would get him out of having to drink it all.

As if she were a preacher in the pulpit—as if she read it from the Bible—Mother grimly said, "Drink it. Bitter in the mouth makes the heart sound."

Eyes shut, holding his nose, he sipped the stuff. It was too hot; otherwise he would have downed it in one dog-gulp, just to be done with it. He gagged again.

"If you gag once more . . . " Mother said sternly. "Well, I warn you. Because if you get any of that medicine on the bed, why, it would eat a hole right through my best quilt that I just threw on top of you, even though you don't deserve it."

"Then won't it eat holes in me?" Moonta asked.

Mother hadn't bothered to answer such a silly question.

Still, it had made it easier to get the cupful down, because Moonta began imagining the medicine eating through him, making his skin full of tiny red-brown pin holes. He'd be spouting and spurting, and bloody all over. It already sort of felt that way, the prickly way he was sweating.

It began to seem so real that after Mother left to return the cup and empty medicine bottle to the kitchen, Moonta took a quick look under the covers. Of course there weren't any red-brown pin holes, nor any blood; but he was so sweaty and steamy under the heap of bedclothes, he could easily imagine that he was a sieve. It almost felt as if he could go swimming in his own steam under the waves of blankets.

It was so still in the living room, Mother was so quiet, just to amuse himself Moonta went on for a while imagining wild things. It kept his mind off his father. Father still had to come home, and then would he catch it. The thought of Father coming and saying things scared him. It was funny, Father most likely wouldn't say nearly as much as Mother had. But he said them in a man's voice, and that made you cringe more. It could make you feel like an absolute fool.

Mother came back into the room. "I'm going out to get some more of that medicine. You stay under those covers."

When Mother returned from the store Moonta knew at once by the way she closed the front door that she'd found out about the draught ditch. He closed his eyes to make her

100

think he was sleeping. It didn't fool Mother. Way from the doorway she said, "There'll be no more skating for you on those ditches. If you're so ashamed to skate with the little beginners that you'd rather take chances of drowning in a draught ditch, there'll be no more skating there for you."

"But, Mother," he pointed out reasonably, "I'm three times bigger than those little beginners, and—" He stopped at once. It wasn't the right thing to say. Instead he said, "Mother, you didn't come. You said you would, but instead the headmaster came. And you weren't sure he didn't have the right to forbid me to skate on the beginners' ditches, and Grandpa wasn't home. . . . Anyway, the headmaster told me right on Main Street that it was all right for me to skate on the beginners' ditches. He said I might since I'm a true beginner, because I was sick that winter."

"Now *I* say you mayn't," Mother said shortly.

"But, Mother," he argued indignantly, "you didn't come, and the other mothers didn't care—they just cared about their own children. They didn't care I'd been sick and had to learn. And . . . and they all blamed me for all their little children falling and tumbling, and they told me to get off that ditch. But you didn't come."

Now at last he'd hit on the right things to say.

"Oh, they did, did they?" Mother said. "And they blamed you? Well, I care about you, and I don't care to have you driven into draught ditches. And I was most certainly there,

101

but I imagine by that time they were already carrying you for a 'pickerel' down Main Street."

"Then, can I go back tomorrow and learn to skate?" Moonta asked. "If you go with me?" he added quickly. "I don't have to hide from the headmaster and go in draught ditches now," he pointed out.

"No," Mother said. "I said No, didn't I? Can't you ever learn that 'No' is a final word?"

Moonta made a face. Sometimes mothers, especially when they were angry and scared, didn't make much sense. "But you said—" he began again.

"No!" Mother said. She turned around and went to the kitchen. Moonta listened, half afraid she was going to make another cup of medicine, but it began to sound more as if she

was starting to make supper. It made Father's coming seem much closer. Moonta sighed.

There now was Father. He came straight on into the living room to Moonta's bed. It turned out far better than Moonta could have expected. Leendert had met Father outside the village and had told him about Moonta's soaking in the draught ditch. But Leendert had taken all the blame

102

for himself and his friends. "He was really sorry" Father told Mother. "I guess Leendert wanted me to hear it from him first," he said to Moonta. "Well, at least that saves me the trouble of digging the real truth out of you."

Mother's mouth was open because Father wasn't being severe. "Father," Moonta said hurriedly, "I can skate, but only when I'm scared. When I was scared of the headmaster and scared of the water, then I could skate; but when I think about it, I can't skate worth two cents."

"I'll say he can't," Mother said. "Do you know when I made him undress to go to bed, he had black-and-blue spots all over his body? He must hurt, although he won't say. He's going at it too hard."

Something boiled over in the kitchen, and Mother had to run. "Father," Moonta said the moment Mother was gone, "may I, if I don't get on that draught ditch again, go skating after supper, in the moonlight? Lees said it was going to be moonlight all week."

Father shook his head. "Sorry, Moonta, no use getting in a quick plea with me. You know how Mother is about pneumonia. It looks like you're going to have to enjoy the moonlight from bed." He started to leave the room.

"Father," Moonta urged, "all the beginners—with their fathers along to teach them—will be learning tonight in the moonlight. But I'll just be lying here. And I'll still be the only one in the village that doesn't know how to skate."

"Looks like you'll have to take up crocheting like your Aunt Cora," Father joked. "I'll bring you a needle and a doily."

Moonta spat. Not really, of course, not in bed, but he made the sound.

"I know," Father said. "And it's a most sorry picture you paint, my mustardy-smelling son; but is there any reason, when ice comes on the canal, you can't learn right on the canal? If it keeps freezing tonight as hard as it froze last night, I'm almost sure that sometime tomorrow we'll have safe ice on the canal. Won't that be a village holiday after four long years?"

"Good ice on the canal already?" Moonta yelped unbelievingly.

Father nodded. "I had to go twenty miles outside the village today—we're going to build a big new school way out there—and do you know that as soon as the canal bends away from the sea the ice begins to get thicker? Inland a few miles the ice actually looked thick enough to skate on—except under the bridges, of course." Father stood thinking. "Hey, maybe tomorrow—if we start far outside the village—your mother and I could even take the Eleven-Towns Tour and hit every town in the province by way of the canals. I wonder . . . we haven't been able to do that for years. Would that be a treat for her!"

Excitement died in Moonta. "Tomorrow," he said, "with ice on the canal, everybody will be skating but me. Even all the beginners will be on the canal, because they'll all learn tonight by moonlight with their fathers. But not me. I'll still be learning all alone on the beginners' ditches, and you and Mother will be gone."

"Sure, sure, you'll be sitting all alone in a ditch like a lone, croaking frog," Father finished for him. "Moonta, didn't I tell you that if there's safe ice, you'll be on the canal to-morrow? You with a little red chair."

"But only babies, only the littlest kids, learn to skate behind little chairs. Who wants to go pushing a chair out ahead of him—and me a fourth grader? Everyone will laugh."

"Son, everybody will be too busy with his own skating and his own fun to be bothered about you."

"But a little chair!"

"I learned with a little chair," Father said. "It didn't do so badly by me, did it? I still think it's the best way to learn. Much better than a big person holding you up in impossible, awkward positions. Certainly far better than smashing your-self black-and-blue against the ice."

"I won't do it," Moonta said.

Father looked at him so long Moonta expected a slap.

But Father didn't lift a hand or raise his voice. "Somehow you remind me of your Aunt Cora," he said slowly. "She learned to skate the same year I did; we were both little kids. But she was big for her age, so she thought she was almost a grown woman, and she absolutely wouldn't skate behind a chair. So she kept turning her ankles and smashing herself black, blue, and bloody-nosed against the ice. All because of her silly, childish pride."

Moonta stayed very quiet. Father stood still, looking away from him across the room. "Well, as you know, your Aunt Cora still can't skate. Her little red chair still stands up in our attic. Your Mother learned with it and turned out to be a champion. Tomorrow, if skating ice comes, it'll be the biggest village holiday in years. The whole village will be on the ice, but your Aunt Cora will be sitting crocheting beside somebody's bed—she'll be a baby-sitter, or a nurse for somebody that's sick. . . . Oh, I must get you that needle and a doily."

There was a long silence in the room. It went on so long, it was so still, Moonta could hear the frying pan sizzle and Mother's quick steps in the kitchen.

Moonta raised his head. "I'll skate with the chair." His face felt hot and red, but that of course was from the heat under the blankets.

"Good, then I'll tell you something. A chair gives you confidence while you're getting your skating legs, while you're getting the feel. Don't kid yourself—every time you smash to the ice a little confidence goes out of you. You start to watch yourself and think about how to move your feet. You told me yourself you only skated when you ran scared, and that's the reason—you weren't thinking about yourself or your skates then."

106

"Tomorrow's Saturday," Moonta said hopefully. "School will be out at noon, and then . . ."

"If there's ice, school will be out all day," Father said. "School is every week, but ice is seldom. You'll see; it'll be one big day-after-day holiday. Nobody will work or go to school. For the few days that there's ice, everybody will be practically living on the canal."

Moonta sighed with yearning.

"I'll tell you what," Father said. "No, I'll even promise it. If there's ice and if by tomorrow evening you've learned to skate without your chair, why, then, after I get back from the Eleven-Towns Tour with Mother, you and I'll still go out by moonlight—all the way to the New Church's Pipe. I'll say, 'Lay on, son,' put my clasped hands on my back, palms up, and you'll lay your hands in mine, and we'll strike out together— you on behind me—and we won't stop until we see the New Church's Pipe in the moonlight. Is that a bargain?"

"Father!" Moonta whispered. "New Church's Pipe," he whispered. He got so warm that even though his father stood right there, he had to throw the quilts back.

"Now remember," Father cautioned, "that promise of mine depends on whether both you and the ice are strong and healthy tomorrow."

Father left. Moonta half reared up in bed to call out after him: "What's the New Church's Pipe? Where is it?" Then he decided he wasn't going to ask at all. If he had to lie in bed the whole long evening, that'd be something to do—to think and wonder about the New Church's Pipe. Work it all out for himself.

Father and Mother both came back into the room, Mother carrying a heaping plate of food. Moonta didn't say anything, but he knew he'd be too excited to eat.

"Your mother and I are going to eat in the kitchen," Father said. "She wants it quiet and dark in here in the hope that after you're full of warm food you'll fall asleep."

Mother made Moonta sit up and adjusted the hot-water crocks around him. "Whew," she said at the waves of mustardy smell that came up from the blankets. Then she grinned most innocently. "Moonta, I forgot to ask, but do you want any mustard on your food?"

Moonta grabbed one of the hot-water crocks and made as if he was going to hurl it at her. Mother ducked. Father grabbed her by the hand and ran with her from the room. Mother laughed and giggled all the way down the hall—she was like a young girl. Father must have told her in the kitchen about the two of them going on the all-day Eleven-Towns Tour, and it was making her act like a girl. Now they were talking and laughing in the kitchen.

Moonta looked at his heaping plate of food. He was too excited; he couldn't eat. Then he dug into the food. He was going to be strong, he wasn't going to be sick tomorrow. He was going to learn with the little red chair how to skate *without* the little red chair. And then Father would say, "Lay on." And the two of them would strike out for the faraway New Church's Pipe, and he wouldn't even know what it was or where it was.

The moon was coming out. Moonlight lay long and still in the room.

The moon was Moonta's punishment the whole long evening in bed, even more than the hot jugs and hot rock and the suffocating pile of hot covers. The villagers made use of the moonlight to keep making clattering trips to the canal to look at the ice. They kept going by the windows of the living room, and from their excited words, clear in the frosty air— clear as the moonlight—Moonta could make out that ice was really forming on the canal—solid, sound, safe ice.

Everybody was getting ready for a big day on the canal. People kept coming to the house, but they went on through the yard to Father's backyard carpenter shop. They hadn't even let Father finish his supper. Now these last hours before ice the whole village still seemed to need to have its skates sharpened. The whine of the grinding wheel sounded without letup from the carpenter shop. The keening, teeth-watering sharp sound of the grinding wheel on the hard steel of the skates shrilled through the house.

When there were pauses, and the grinding wheel oozed down to slowness and silence, then in the clear, still air

Moonta in bed could hear the sounds from the ditches of the Children's Skate School Field. The excited sounds seemed almost words you could understand, but they weren't; they were fun and excitement. Moonta listened and lay in pure woe. It must be that the fathers and mothers and big brothers and sisters were out there in the moonlight, helping the shrilling little kids to skate. And here he lay.

Mother briefly peeked into the room. She had her shawl thrown over her head. "I've just got to run out to the canal a minute to see how that ice is coming in the moonlight. I'll tell you all about it, but stay under those covers."

As the front door fell shut, and he was sure she wouldn't hear, Moonta called out after Mother, "What's the New Church's Pipe? Where is it? How far away?" Somehow, doing it that way helped him not to ask outright so he'd get an answer. If he knew, there'd be nothing to do and think about the whole long evening and night.

After Mother had gone down the street, Moonta thought about dashing to the attic—just for a few quick moments— to look for the little red chair. He didn't do it. He did put the flat palms of his hands under the covers. He raised them high to let a little cool air stream over him. He didn't do it long. He tucked everything tightly around him again; he just couldn't take chances. What if he were sick tomorrow, what if he got pneumonia or even a cold? The thought was awful.

He imagined it to himself. Why, then it would be exactly

as it had been four winters ago. Exactly. Everybody out on the ice and Aunt Cora sitting on a chair below the bed, reading a book to him. He pushed himself down under the covers up to his nose.

Just so as not to think about being sick, he decided that when Mother got back he'd ask outright about the New Church's Pipe. No, he wasn't going to ask even Father. Not even at that great moment tomorrow when the two of them would start out—he and Father.

No, even at that great moment he wouldn't ask. Father would put his clasped hands on the small of his back and say, "Lay on, Moonta." Then they'd stroke away. Long, straight, together-swaying strokes, like real skaters. A long stroke here, a long stroke there—strokes ten, twenty feet long without moving a foot. It would be like gliding over the ice. They would be like gulls in the air, the way gulls used the air without flapping their wings. They'd be gulls on ice—they'd be like eagles. They'd be two dark figures going far out a long white-ice canal; two figures looking like one, swaying like one, farther and farther, and then at last in the loneliest of the far distances, there—rising up—would be the New Church's Pipe.

At a little sound Moonta whipped around, eager for it to be Mother. He reminded himself not to ask about the New Church's Pipe. He had to remember—he wasn't going to ask her.

111

Now the front door opened. Moonta quickly tucked the whole secret down deep inside him as Mother came in. He shoved it down just as if he'd been reading a forbidden book and was shoving it out of sight under the covers. It felt that real.

"There'll be ice, oh, there'll be ice tomorrow," Mother sang out from the hall. She came in. "Imagine, Moonta, tomorrow about this time your father and I'll be coming back into the village from the Eleven-Towns Tour. And you'll be there skating in the moonlight on the village end of the canal—our whole little family on the ice."

End of the canal, Moonta thought to himself derisively. Why, he'd be on his way with Father to the New Church's Pipe. He did not dare say anything out loud to Mother. He didn't dare, for it was as if he could feel the three words— New Church's Pipe—right behind his teeth, as if only his teeth were holding them in. He clenched his teeth on the words.

In the stillness they could hear the grinding wheel begin its slow, gather-speed moan. "Oh, that reminds me," Mother said. "Our own skates! They never get sharpened, your father's always so busy with everybody else's. Now where can they be?"

"Mine, too," Moonta said eagerly.

"They shouldn't be dull yet, should they?" Mother asked

112

doubtfully. "Oh, all right. You're now part of this skating family." She bustled away.

It was so exciting that the only way Moonta could be still was to duck back into his dreaming about the New Church's Pipe. He imagined it as being round. Not thin round, thick round. Not a thin length of pipe, but more like a silo, except much higher—high like a tower. No, not a round tower either —more like a monument. Yes, a monument rising all by itself in a flat field before a village—maybe even at the edge of a town. It stood out in a loneness far out a long, lone canal.

He kept picturing it still more exactly. It was like making a drawing of a dream. You didn't really know anything about it, but still in your mind there it was, and it took shape and it kept adding—almost as if you were building it.

Father came in with three pairs of skates. "Well, I hope these are the last and we three are my last customers. Man, I'm tired." He grinned. "That'll cost you half a guilder, Moonta. I had work with those. That's a good pair of skates— real hard steel."

Moonta glowed with pride, as if he had made the skates.

Father laid the three pairs of skates carefully on a chair so as not to cut the seat. They must be very sharp. Moonta watched. He didn't know if it was an accident, but there the skates lay—Father's and Mother's with his smaller ones in between them.

Mother called out from the kitchen, "Did you sharpen mine, too?"

"Only one," Father yelled back. "Can't have you skating circles around me tomorrow. Only one."

"Father," Moonta said, "when we get to the New Church's Pipe—you and I, tomorrow . . ."

"Now remember," Father said, "that depends if you learn to skate and if there's good ice. Don't get yourself too excited. Nothing's sure yet."

Moonta made an impatient motion with his head. Here in bed it was easy to imagine himself a good skater. In his mind he'd been skating for hours, better and better, and faster and faster. It had all worked itself out, in between imagining the wondrous, mysterious New Church's Pipe, because of course to get to the Pipe you'd have to be able to skate hard, long, and expertly. Hard and long—and there in the distance far out the long canal would rise the New Church's Pipe.

"The New Church's Pipe . . ." Moonta began.

"For one sharp skate I've made just one cup of strong, hot coffee," Mother called out from the kitchen.

"What's for two?" Father called back.

"Come and see," Mother answered.

Father picked up both her skates from the chair, and that sort of spoiled the picture of the way they would skate some-day—their whole little family, him in between—but of course Father didn't know.

114

"Tomorrow's going to be a hard day for you," Father said, "learning to skate and then the same day going out to the New Church's Pipe. I can tell you that seldom happens to any beginner, so you'd better get to sleep."

"I will, Father," Moonta solemnly promised, and solemnly he closed his eyes as Father left the room. But closing his eyes made mind-pictures flash behind his tight eyelids. The pictures that came were right out of his fourth-grade geography book. They came so clearly, Moonta could even see what it said in print under the pictures. "Cleopatra's Needle—London, England," he read as if he had the geography book open before him. Right across the page was another picture, and the exact words under it: "The Washington Monument—Washington, D.C., the United States of America."

It was silly, of course. The New Church's Pipe wouldn't be anything famous like Cleopatra's Needle or the Washington Monument. It wasn't that important. It wouldn't even be a monument, or anything anybody would put a picture of in a geography book. Still, there it rose behind his closed eyelids as clearly as the geography pictures from the book. It rose round and tall with a blunt, flattish roof, far out a long, lone canal. Two lone figures of skaters, dark on the white ice in the moonlight, swayed toward it in a rhythm of long gliding strokes.

A ghastly thought struck Moonta. What if the New Church's Pipe was just a point to go to on the canal—just a marker? What if it were nothing but a length of pipe driven

115

into the ground? Father would say to him: "Well, here we are." And there it would be—a piece of pipe, maybe to tie a canal boat to, maybe just for a cow to be tied to in a pasture.

He refused to think that one thought further—it was too awful. He was glad that Father and Mother came into the room to go to bed. Mother pushed the doors of his bed somewhat shut so she could undress. Fortunately she had left them open enough so that he could see the moonlight behind the blank, blind, frosted windows. He couldn't see through the windows, and still it was as if he could see a faraway long white ribbon of ice that was a canal, and far out the long canal rose the black roundness of the New Church's Pipe.

Mother was climbing into bed. "Aren't you going to close the shutters?" she asked Father.

"Hey, I'm undressed," Father yelped, "and I'm not pulling everything on again to run around outside and close some shutters. The frost will have to be the shutters."

"Father," Moonta asked, "is Mother going with us to the New Church's Pipe?"

"Nope," Father said. "That's just for the men of this family."

Mother didn't make any sputtering joke, or anything. It must be she'd already fallen asleep. Just he and Father were going. It was just as he had pictured it, and it seemed a proud thing that somehow added to the mystery of the New Church's Pipe.

116

"Father," he started again. But Father was already snoring. Moonta sighed. Grown-ups never stayed excited for long— not even about skating and ice. Well, let them snore, but he was going to stay awake the whole night in the moonlight.

Eleven-Towns Tour

IN THE early morning it was sure that there was ice—safe skating ice covering all the canal. The tower bell announced it. The hoarse, powerful bell in the clock tower boomed out the news, even though it was dark. The moon had gone down in the night. Moonta had not stayed awake in the moonlit night. He had not stayed awake at all—not a moment.

Awakened by the bell, Moonta knelt on his bed. He had shoved the two doors of his bed wide open. He pushed himself out of the bed as far as possible, for now under the boom and growl of the tower bell he heard the brassy tinkle of the hand bell of Evert, the announcer.

Evert must still be out on Main Street. He stopped about every fifth house, silenced his bell, and chanted out a long announcement about good skating ice on the canal. Far as he leaned out of bed, Moonta could not hear all that Evert was chanting—there was too much noise in the village. It was early, dark morning, but it almost seemed as if the villagers had been waiting fully clothed behind their doors for the news that the big bell boomed out and that Evert was chanting.

It must be sharp-cold outside. The voices of the people almost rang out like bells. Excited yells came from everywhere. Wooden shoes clattered hard over the frozen cobblestone streets. It seemed everybody was outside; everybody was running to see the ice on the canal.

Now to his amazement Moonta became aware that there wasn't a sound from the other bed. He turned an impatient head, but he couldn't see around the opened bed door. How could they sleep on? It was amazing how grown-ups could stay so unexcited.

Then Moonta thought of it. He wasn't sick. He wasn't sick at all. He hadn't got pneumonia or anything. He was healthy and hungry and excited.

Now Evert and his bell came jangling up Moonta's own

street. Suddenly Moonta didn't care what his parents would say when they woke up. He had to hear what Evert was chanting. Moonta grabbed the edge of the bed and swung himself out. He started to poke in the dark for his felt slippers below the bed, but now Evert had stopped just down the street—probably in front of Lees's house. Moonta couldn't be bothered about the slippers. He charged to the front door and rammed it open, both halves together.

There were people in the street—even Lees. She wasn't married, but Moonta didn't care; he stood there in his nightgown, barefooted on the edge of the ice stoop. Lees looked at him, shook her head, but didn't say anything, because just then Evert was beginning his announcement.

"There is ice—safe, sound, skating ice—except under some bridges," Evert sang out. "And the water holes along the canal will be roped off during the course of the day. But everywhere else the ice is so safe that a school holiday has been declared by Headmaster Andries. A school holiday.

"There will be no school this Saturday morning, and if the ice lasts, no school on Monday. After that there will only be half days of school as long as the ice lasts. All scholars are expected to make up this free time by going to school on their Wednesday and Saturday half holidays for the rest of the winter.

"Hear this, hear this—one and all. An ice holiday has been declared."

Evert started forward, jangling his bell again, but when he saw Moonta barefooted on the stoop, he grabbed his bell by its clapper and said, "Get inside, boy. Get inside. You aren't going to be able to skate on a mess of chilblains."

Moonta stepped back into the hall and closed the bottom door, but not the top half. He didn't answer Evert; he was too excited. But then he just had to yell out across the street: "Lees, Lees, it's just as you said. Ice before Sunday. Will it stay? Will it stay, Lees?"

Lees laughed. "It'll last, at least, today, Moonta. Let's take it a day at a time, shall we? Look, as it is you're going to have to make up all this free time by going to school Wednesdays and Saturdays—maybe the whole winter long."

"I'd go to school on Sundays, Moonta said fervently. "I'd go for a year. Just so there's ice and I learn to skate."

"Then get inside and close that door, and get some clothes on, and something on your feet," Lees ordered. "You don't want to spend a week of ice in bed again, like that other winter, do you?"

It sobered Moonta. He immediately reached out to pull the upper half-door shut, but he had trouble. Lees started across the street to help him. At that moment the kitchen door at the other end of the hall opened, and there stood Grandpa.

Grandpa was here. Moonta hadn't known. Now with the kitchen door open he could hear Father and Mother talking to Grandpa. They were up, and Grandpa was here!

121

Mother asked loudly, "Moonta isn't outside? Make him come in this minute. Tell him to close that door—fast."

At that moment Lees shoved the upper door shut behind Moonta. Moonta raced toward Grandpa. It was a marvel. Early as it was, there stood Grandpa, and his skates were sticking out of his overcoat pocket. "Grandpa!" he yelled. But then he remembered, doubled back, shot his feet into his slippers, and came racing down the hall again. He was glad he'd remembered in time; Mother had sharp eyes—she'd have seen his bare feet the first thing—she never missed anything.

Grandpa still waited in the kitchen doorway. Moonta put a finger on his lips and pointed to his slippers. Grandpa understood; he winked. Oh, you could tell it was a terribly important day in that Grandpa had come. Grandfather seldom came to their house, only when there was bad or great news. And here was Grandpa this early morning, with his skates in his pocket.

"There's ice, there's ice, there's ice," Moonta sang out as he burst into the kitchen.

Mother and Father were sitting eating breakfast—imagine, he hadn't known; he'd thought they were still asleep. Grandpa must have already had breakfast; he stayed standing up in his overcoat. Now he pulled his skates out of his pocket. "Mind you—that comes from getting old—I totally forgot to get my skates sharpened," Grandpa said to Father. "That's why I came plenty early. Thought you could sharpen my skates,

122

and then you and I could still make the Eleven-Towns Tour of the whole province today. You never know how long ice will last, and you, being the skater you are, Riemer Riemersma, even though I'll slow you down, I thought I could still do the tour with you—for a last time. May not get back home till midnight, but I sort of got my heart set on it."

Moonta stood stock-still in the doorway. He went cold, but this cold was from the inside out.

"What about me?" Mother was saying indignantly to Grandpa. "Don't you want me along? I've been counting on

123

that tour too. I'm just as good a skater as your Riemer Riemersma—even if I am your daughter."

"Hey," Grandpa said. "That would be better yet. A last tour in my old age before I put my skates away forever—a family tour with you and Riemer."

"But what about me?" Moonta screamed it out from the doorway. He didn't care that Grandpa whirled on him, and that they all looked startled. "What about me? Father was going to take me to the New Church's Pipe, but now he won't because you'll be gone till midnight."

Father's hand came up. He said nothing; he just pointed. Moonta didn't wait. He knew what Father was going to say: "Cry babies in bed."

He raced down the hall and threw himself so hard, high up against the bed, it hurt his knee, but he didn't care. In bed he kneeled, kicked out like a mule, and sent his slippers flying. He pulled all the blankets over himself—way over his head. The big tower bell still tolled on; he could hear it through the thickness of the blankets. He shoved his fingers in his ears.

The blankets were jerked down from around him. It was Father. Moonta whirled over and buried his face in the pillow. He didn't want to do it—not with Father. But how could he explain all he had pictured and dreamed of the New Church's Pipe? And now it wouldn't be. And if the ice didn't hold, maybe it would never be.

"Sit up, look at me, and listen to me," Father said quietly.

To Moonta's sullen surprise Father seemed more sad than angry. "I came in here," Father said, "because I know your grandfather would give up the last Eleven-Towns Tour of his life for you, if you yammered about it long enough before him.

"Look at me! Your grandfather ought not to go on that stiff tour; he shouldn't do it. And dragging him from town to town is all but going to kill even a skater like me, but I'm going to do it for him even if it kills me. Because, Moonta, it's going to be his very last trip. You're at the beginning of life, and for you skating with me to the Pipe would be a first thing, but first things are followed by other things. For your grandfather the tour will be a last thing—forever. Do you understand?"

Moonta rocked himself and wouldn't answer a word.

"I know you had your heart set on it," Father said, "but you should give up the trip—not your grandpa. Do you know that if you let him give up that tour for you, that all your life you'd be sorry? You love him, but will you believe me if I tell you that you'll love him all the more if you give up your trip so he may have his? It works that way, even if I don't know how to explain it to you."

Moonta sat knuckling his eyes, but he understood. Inside he felt the meaning of Father's words.

"I know, Father," he said at last, but the ache in his throat made the words come out bitter and stiff. "I know, but I still have to learn to skate, and it was going to be so great, and . . .

and now I'll be here alone learning to skate, the only one with a little chair. . . . Even the littlest kids learned on the ditches last night."

"No, you're losing sight of your grandpa again, you're so full of your own woes," Father said sternly. "There's only one thing you've got to keep in your mind: For your grandpa it's a sort of a last day."

"It's all right, Father," Moonta said, taking his knuckles away from his eyes, hoping his eyes weren't too silly red. With his knuckles in his eyes, he hadn't noticed that Mother had come into the room and was standing there quietly listening. "Moonta," she said, "I've decided I'm not going. I'll be here. I'll be skating at the village end of the canal, too. Nobody will know but you and me, but I'll be keeping an eye on you. The moment I see you're ready to skate without your chair, why, I'll toss it up on the deck of one of the canal boats, and away you and I will go."

"To the New Church's Pipe?" Moonta demanded.

"Well, now. That I don't know. "You still have to learn, but it's a long day, and we'll see."

Oh, he loved Mother. She could be so strict and stern and impatient, but here—just like that—she'd just given up her big Eleven-Towns Tour. Moonta knew it was a famous thing to do. Only the very best skaters could do the tour in one day. Oh, he loved her.

Father said, soft-voiced, to Mother, "Do you think you're doing the right thing?"

Mother shrugged.

"Well," Father said shortly, "then if I've got to drag the old man around the province alone, we'd best be going."

He might have said more, but Grandfather came down the hall. He stopped in the doorway. "What's all this family whispering and confabbing about? And get that kid out of bed, and a big breakfast into him. He's got a big day ahead. But, well—I guess it's a big day for all of us."

"Oh, Father, I've decided I'm not going—it's really men's work, that tour," Mother said hastily. "I thought I should help Moonta learn today. If a thaw should come and he hadn't learned, then he'd still have to learn next year. And as you know, by next year he'll be as old as you are now."

Grandpa grinned. "Yeah, and that's old. But I understand," he said disappointedly. "Here," he said to Father, "we've still got to sharpen my skates." Father ran his thumb expertly along the blades. "These are as sharp as an assassin's knife," he announced. "They can't be any sharper."

"That's right," Grandfather said. "I forgot—I had them sharpened the last two winters all for nothing. I just couldn't find any ice, and I didn't want to walk to Outer Siberia."

Suddenly he sobered and said to Moonta, "When I get back tonight, if I've still got the strength, I'm going to give you a spanking. You acting up until your mother felt she had to give up her tour with your father and me! So wait up for me. . . . And you, Riemer, you go get your jacket; let's go."

Mother quickly bustled about. She came in with an old cracked teapot. Out of it she dug a handful of halfpennies and gave them to Grandpa and Father. "For the sweepers," she announced. "There's been a little snow, so they'll be sweeping the ice, need it or not, and if you don't toss a coin they'll toss their brooms between your feet. I'd hate you to go down with broken bones, Father."

"Will there be some for us?" Moonta inquired anxiously. "If we should go to the New Church's Pipe?"

"There's plenty," Mother said. "There should be; I've been saving them for this all these iceless winters. . . . Watch it, you two," she ordered Father and Grandpa. "Stop off at one of those tents they'll have set up along the canals and buy yourselves an orange, or hot chocolate, or buns with cheese. You can get so gape-hungry sick, skating hard in this bitter cold. So remember to stop before you get the yawning ice-hunger. And have a big day."

"We will, we will," they both promised like little boys.

"Yes, and you two watch yourselves too," Father now ordered in turn. "Don't stand around sweaty. And have a big day." Then he and Grandpa turned down the hall.

"You too," Moonta yelled after them. "You too, Grandpa. Have a great day."

128

From the doorway Grandpa turned to give him a huge wink. "You just get up. Nobody, just nobody as yet has ever learned to skate in bed. And if it should happen that this isn't my last tour, next year I'll expect to do it with you and your mother along. No, by golly, this isn't going to be my last tour—next year is, when we can do it with all of us as a family."

Moonta got on his knees, pushed himself out of bed as far as he could, to watch Father and Grandpa go by past the windows. When they passed he once more yelled: "Have a great day!" Then he put his hands on Mother's shoulders, reached around and kissed her. "I love you, Mother."

"It's nothing but ice love, and that's worse than cupboard love," Mother said. "It's much colder. But from you I love any kind of love. Let's get you a big steaming breakfast, and strength for a long day on the ice."

9

Canal Holiday

SOMEHOW Moonta's nervous fingers, fumbling with every button, at last got him dressed. It was taking five times too long. After that he was as clumsy as a baby with its first shoestring. He fumbled and fumbled, then just tied both shoestrings with knots. Mother was making the beds. She had climbed on a chair, and was tucking in the corners of the one high bed with a square measuring stick. She happened to glance down, saw Moonta tying his shoestrings in knots. She made him tie them properly. "If they dangle," she said, "a skate cutting through a loose shoestring can give you a nasty fall. It could send you right over your little chair, and while that would be wonderful acrobatics, it's not good skating."

Moonta grumped, and did as he was told.

"My, I'm glad you didn't get pneumonia," Mother said. "You're not hiding it? You're really not sick? Maybe you're not feeling anything because you're so excited at going skating."

"I'm fine," Moonta said.

"Well, then—your porridge is standing ready on the kitchen table, and two good stiff hunks of black bread with cheese. That should fortify you for at least part of the morning. Oh, I'm glad you're feeling fine. You're not hiding anything?"

Moonta straightened from his shoe-tying job, made an impatient motion with his head, and rushed to the kitchen.

As he hitched his chair to the table, the steam from the hot bowl of porridge curled up around his nose. He gagged. He couldn't eat—he was all jelly inside; he was quivering. He retched at the thick, sweet smell of the porridge, and looked about to see if there was any place he could dump it where Mother wouldn't find it. There wasn't any place. Instead he jumped up and ran to the living room to get his skates. He

131

laid the skates on the table; maybe it would help him to eat if he kept his eyes on the skates. It didn't help. He gagged from the smell of the curly steam. He jumped up again, found a piece of newspaper, and frumpled it around the thick slices of bread and cheese, and ran to his jacket and shoved them in the pocket.

Now at least he wouldn't have to eat those. It was even good. If he got the sick gape-hunger on the ice, he'd have something to cure it.

Moonta got back to his chair just in time. Mother came into the kitchen. She shoved his chair farther under the table. Now his whole face was over the sickening porridge. He tried hard to keep from retching. "I put extra sugar in it—that makes for pep, strength, and energy," Mother said cheerily. "Now I'll get dressed for skating, and then we'll go out to the canal. Except for eating, not a lick more of housework all day. It's to be a complete holiday on the canal. So spoon up that porridge."

He turned unwillingly back to the porridge, but he felt so sick he lied right out to Mother—outrageously. "I ate the bread," he said, "but, Mother, I can't eat any porridge. I can't."

"It's the excitement," Mother said. "We'll leave it for noon —you watch yourself wolf it then. Bundle up well. There's nothing worse than standing around on ice all sweated up."

"I'm not going to stand; I'm going to skate," he said smartly.

Fortunately Mother was too busy getting herself ready to

notice he was being smart. But after he was in his jacket and muffler and stocking cap, she really examined him. She pulled and tugged, and straightened and ordered things. Then she grabbed her skates.

Moonta grabbed his skates and dashed ahead of her. "Race you down the hall," he yelled.

"I'm a dignified old lady," Mother joked. "I don't race down halls, but I'll race you on the ice."

"Next year," he said. "Next year I'll beat the stuffings right out of you."

"What an expression to use to a dignified old lady," Mother said, coming on slowly, walking very straight—just to tease him.

Moonta had the outer door open and held it for Mother. "Now that's proper treatment," Mother said. But she stopped doubtfully in the doorway. "Hey, wind," she said. "Where's it coming from, over land or over sea? That's important for continuing ice. If the wind shifts . . ."

Moonta looked anxiously across the street. Ah, Lees was there, leaning over her half door. "Lees, what about the wind?" he yelled. "Is it shifting? Will the ice last?"

"It may, or it may not," Lees said, looking up at the sky. I've got a lot of sewing to do, but I'm thinking of sneaking in a little skating tomorrow—outside the village, of course. I could do that better than sew on Sunday—my rattly old sewing machine gives me away."

133

Everything settled in Moonta, everything seemed better now. If Lees figured on skating tomorrow, well, then, there'd be ice tomorrow. Mother must have figured the same way, for she closed the door and set the broom upside down against it to show there was nobody home. Then she thought of it. "Oh, we forgot your little red chair," she said. "It's up in the attic."

Moonta shoved his skates into Mother's hands, knocked the broom down, yanked both door halves open, and tore back into the house.

"It's too cold to stand still," Mother called after him. "I'll walk on, and you can catch up with me—you've got eager, young legs."

Up in the attic Moonta didn't look about, but tore into the mass of things piled tier on tier against the end wall. The high pile was an assortment of everything. Everything except a red chair. Moonta wildly tugged at things, hoping that behind some box or bunched bedding he'd catch a glimpse of something red. Then an old, moth-eaten feather bed sagged away from the wall, folded in the middle as if it had a terrible stomach ache, sagged to the floor. There was the little red chair! It had been propped under the soft feather bed to hold it against the wall. Moonta waded over the billowy bed—it was almost like wading in water—and grabbed the chair.

He gave the whole untidy, tumbled mess one glance and a hopeless shrug of his shoulder, and lunged down the stairway with his chair. At the foot of the stairs he looked back and carefully closed the stairway door.

Outside he didn't bother about setting the broom upside down against the closed door. People would know they weren't home—nobody was home this day, everybody was on the canal. You could hear them screaming and yelling and shrilling. Nobody was home—he was the only one, all because of the miserable chair.

Moonta raced down the street. It had taken him so long to find the chair, he didn't catch up with Mother until he got to the Main Street end of the canal.

"Well, that took you long," Mother said.

"It was way back under everything," Moonta panted.

"Sure, and I suppose you let it all lie as it fell—for me to pick up later."

Moonta bleakly nodded. He had no words. He stood astounded and open-mouthed. He felt dismayed and let down. Everybody, the whole village—young and old—everybody was on the ice. The canal was black with squirming, squiggling, racing people. It looked mad. People skated everywhere in every direction, and yelled and shouted and laughed and sang. It was unbelievable that they didn't crash and tumble all over each other and land in heaps. Long lines of twenty to thirty people behind each other, hands clasped, came bearing down on other long snaking lines. Miraculously they always missed each other, swept around each other, whiplashed in great snaking curves around still other lines, then swung and swayed in an excitement of bodies and noise and dark clothes on white ice.

In the midst of all the long dangerous-looking lines, people singly or in pairs calmly went skating on their own way, to some point that only they knew. All kinds of little kids were scooting and scratching and scrambling around. People shot up the canal, down the canal, across the canal, and on long crisscrossing slants and even in and out among the canal boats frozen into the ice. The end of the canal was so crowded there did not seem room for one more skater. Certainly there was no room for a chair.

"Look at it, look at it," Mother said. "They're starved for skating, they're giddy with it. Everybody's been yelling up at me while I stood here. They don't care what they say; they don't even know. Everything is fun.

Moonta said nothing. He stared in dismay.

"I must say, I've been standing here dithering myself," Mother said. "I'm all quirky and little jiggles keep running up my legs to get on the ice. I thought you'd never come."

With Mother talking about her jiggly feet, Moonta noticed she had already tied her skates on. Now she let herself down the bank. She reached up her arms, "First hand me your chair, then hand me you."

Moonta held back. "I'm not going down there. Mother,

there's nobody skating with chairs, just two little kids that still can't do anything but skate on their ankles. They're not half as big as I am." He eyed all the darkness of the people, the whirl and the weaving and the wild, noisy busyness. He looked at the row of seven canal boats. "Mother," he asked in a small voice, "couldn't we start beyond the canal boats, there aren't nearly so many people there. There isn't room here."

Mother frowned. "Nonsense," she said firmly. "It may look that way from the top of the bank, but you'll see when you get down here with me that there's plenty of room. You'll see —people will make way; you won't run into them or they into you."

At that moment a line of thirty or forty boys—from the fifth and sixth grades in school—came driving straight toward Mother. The end of the fierce skating line whipped in such a tight sweep around Mother that her skirts rippled and billowed out. The boys dug in their sharp skate heels and scraped to a halt in a fine high spray of ice dust and snow. Even before the whole line had stopped they were all yelling: "Mrs. Riemersma, where's Riemer? Where's your husband? We want him to lead our line."

"He's gone on the Eleven-Towns Tour," Mother said.

"Oh, then will you lead us? Please?" They crowded around Mother. "Please, we're having a race with the men, and we want to race the young fellows too. And maybe with you in the lead we'll win. We've got the master with us—he's the tail end, but he's holding us back. He's a drag and an anchor, so we need you to lead."

Moonta looked on with alarmed eyes. There behind the whole tight group of boys was the headmaster. He stood, breathing too hard to say anything. He took off his woolen cap, and steam actually came up from under it. Moonta was astounded to hear the boys talk that way about the headmaster where he could hear every word they said. Anything seemed to go on the ice.

"Yes, Mrs. Riemersma," the headmaster panted. "You lead them, won't you? They ought to win at least once from the old men. With me all they can beat is some women, and they've been trying so hard."

Then the headmaster noticed Moonta up on the bank with the red chair. "Hey, Moonta," he said. "Going to teach your mother skating? I see you brought a chair."

Everybody laughed. Moonta colored and felt small and silly. Mother looked at him. At last he managed to stammer, "Oh, no, Master, I'm teaching the little red chair."

"Don't 'Master' me today, Moonta," the headmaster ordered. "Today I'm one of the boys—except that they say I'm nothing but an old rusty anchor. . . . What do you say—if you loan them your Mother, and I stop being their anchor—that you and I go skate together with the chair? Is that a fair deal? Fellows, listen," he yelled to the babbling, crowding big graders around Mother. "Listen a minute, will you? Moonta's giving you the loan of his mother, to beat the old men and maybe even the young fellows in a good race. Moonta's still got to learn to skate, because he was sick the last winter we had ice. Hey, that seems long ago—I was younger then; nobody was calling me a drag anchor then."

They yelled back jokes at the headmaster, they yelled up at Moonta all kinds of excited, bright, crazy things. The headmaster lifted Moonta down, chair and all. Nobody laughed at him or poked fun; they all thought it so wonderful that they could have Mother as the leader of their line.

Then Mother was saying to them, "Lay on, lay on." They all stopped their kidding and quickly formed a line by putting clasped hands behind their backs for the one behind to grasp.

"It's all right, isn't it, Moonta?" Mother called over her shoulder as the line started slowly away. Her cheeks were red with excitement. "You'll be in good hands."

"Sit down on that chair and I'll tie your skates, and then I'll watch you skate to see if they need any adjustment to one side or the other," the headmaster ordered.

To Moonta's amazement, when the headmaster had finished he wanted to try the little chair. He had to bend over nearly double, he stuck out behind most undignified, but he went skating away with the little red chair straight across the canal, right in among the thickest crowd. He made a great loop, then came swooping back where Moonta stood plastered up against the canal bank.

As he neared Moonta the headmaster sent the chair flying
and twisting over the ice. "Try it," he yelled. "Moonta, this is
it! What I wouldn't have given for a little chair like this when
I had to learn to skate. But in the part of the country where I
was born, I guess nobody had the brains to think of such a
simple way to learn. . . . Try it, you've got to try it."

Moonta caught the little chair on the fly, grabbed a tight
hold on the back, and like that he was skating. He was skating,
he was skating! He went in a big loop just like the headmaster
had done, and then he came back straight at the master. "Oh,
it's so easy, Master; it's just like that," he yelled.

140

"Isn't it?" the headmaster said. "But don't you 'Master' me today, I said, not on the ice." He skated beside Moonta; they went straight down the canal. It was miraculous, for while from the high bank it looked to be impossible to find even a square yard of room for himself and the chair, now somehow people that were in the way weren't there when he and the chair got there.

When once in a while Moonta got in people's way, they just swirled dizzily around him, or braked by digging their sharp skate heels into the ice.

Nobody poked fun at the chair, nobody even thought of poking fun. Of course that might have been because the headmaster was skating with him. Still it didn't seem so. People that on the streets took off their caps to the headmaster, here on the ice just yelled anything out at him as he skated past. And the headmaster yelled back anything that came into his head. It seemed anything went on the ice.

Now Moonta excitedly twisted his head back to see how far they had come. Then when he turned back, an old man was in the chair's way. He did not get out of the way as fast as Moonta had expected; he was stiff and slow. The headmaster grabbed the chair, swirled Moonta and chair around in a tight circle—if he hadn't, Moonta would have knocked the old man down. Instead Moonta and chair and headmaster went down in a heap and a tangle, but not the old man. He hadn't

141

noticed anything. Now he stopped in surprise and looked down on the fallen headmaster.

"Master," he said, " you down there? But that's what comes of bringing furniture on the ice."

Moonta held his breath, but the headmaster just laughed as he scrambled to his feet and didn't even blame Moonta. In a way he blamed the old man. "Siebren," he said, "I can see you didn't learn with a chair. In fact, I know, because like me, you're from another part of the country. But I can tell you if you had learned with a chair you could have got out of our way in time. Why, man, Monday I'll be here skating on behind the lectern from my schoolroom."

Old man Siebren looked up at the sky. He wet his thumb and held it up. "That lectern might not be a bad idea by Monday," he said. "But bring a couple of oars, too; you'll be sitting in it and using it as a boat. Mark my word, the wind's shifting to the wrong corner. By Monday this canal will be water again."

The headmaster just grinned. "I can't stand weather prophets," he said. "Especially old ones that can't get out of our way." He took hold of Siebren. "Come on, old man, let's you and me strike out for the bend of the canal beyond the village and get out from underfoot. And I'll bet you in another hour or so this Moonta will come racing past us—without a chair."

It was wonderful now. Oh, it was exciting, skating on alone. Moonta had only to remember not to keep looking at the wonder of his flying feet, and of his skates stroking across the ice. It *was* a flying feeling.

Just ahead of him a long line of young women—why, it was Af in the lead—went down in a terrible heap right beside the headmaster and old Siebren. One of them reached out and clawed herself upright by pulling herself up by the headmaster. He lost his balance and went down among the heap of women. He scrambled to his feet, stood over them, and hooted: "What a clumsy bunch of old women."

"Old women!" the young women screeched as they scrambled up. "Why, we're hardly out of your musty old school. . . . Grab him, girls," Af was shrieking. "Grab him, put him in the middle of our line. We'll teach him, we'll make him skate with us 'old women.' "

The headmaster had no chance at all. The line re-formed, he was put in the middle. They swooped away with him in their midst. Everybody that saw it hooted and yelped and cat-called.

Old man Siebren had stayed on his feet. He still stood there looking bewildered and shaking his head. Moonta skated up to him with the red chair. Boldly he asked the old man, "Will you please watch my chair just a moment?"

Before slow old Siebren could think what to say, Moonta skated away without the chair. For thirty, forty, fifty strokes it went fine, then Moonta smashed hard to the ice. He had to lie still for a long moment in surprise and shock. Then, looking alongside himself, he saw one of his shoestrings was dangling. It had caught under his skate. It was nearly cut in two. Moonta angrily yanked the cut piece away, at the same time glad and relieved it was the shoestring that had made him fall. He scrambled to his feet, hoping Siebren hadn't seen him. Then he noticed Siebren wasn't where he had left him. He had skated away. Old as he was, now he was trying the chair.

Moonta raced after him, but when he caught up, the old man didn't give up the chair. Moonta had to skate beside Siebren the way the headmaster had skated beside him. It was a proud wonder. Old Siebren kept saying, "If I could only bend better, boy. This is the thing, this is the thing. Guess I'll have to get me a lectern, like the master—or a sawhorse, or something."

Just then Mother and her whole line of boys came bearing down on them in a fury of skating. As she swept by, Mother called out, "Having fun, Moonta? Having fun?"

"Teaching Siebren, now," Moonta yelled back.

The long line ripped by. It actually felt as if the ice yielded and bent, almost rippled a little from their weight. In a flash Mother was gone. But the last boy in the line, the biggest sixth grader, turned his head. He yelled out at Moonta as he snaked and whipped along, "We beat the men, we're going out to find the young fellows now. We'll beat them for you, Moonta. They're the ones that made you a 'pickerel.'"

"Beat the living daylights out of them," Moonta yelled back. "Beat them hollow. Chase them under the bridge into the water hole. Drown them." He didn't mean it at all; it was just that everything was so exciting, it was something exciting to yell. It made him seem a part of them. He stood and watched them out of sight—enviously. But old Siebren had skated on with the chair; he had to take out after Siebren again. He scratched and he scrabbled.

This time the old man gave up the chair. It felt good to lean on it again. Now with his chair Moonta dared to skate faster and faster. He practiced quick shifts and darts, loops and circles. Then he even dared to take it and weave in and out among the thickest crowd at the Main Street end of the canal.

When he looked up, there was Aunt Cora standing on the high bank. She was watching everything so hard she didn't see him. He skated toward her until he stood right below her. "Aunt Cora," he yelled, "Aunt Cora, oh, this is fun. I'm learning to skate, and I can skate without my chair. Watch my chair, will you? I'll show you." He shoved the chair against the bank and skated away into the thick of the crowd. He felt himself skating so well he couldn't resist—anxious to see that Aunt Cora was watching him—throwing a look up over his shoulder. Like that he smashed to the ice. He'd been looking back, there wasn't time to throw up his hands. He hit the ice flat with his face.

He slowly lifted his head, looked alongside himself, but this time he had not cut a shoestring. His laces were tied. He lay shamed, angry, and mortified. Right before Aunt Cora he'd smashed down like a fool.

"Moonta, Moonta," Aunt Cora cried. "Are you hurt?"

He yelled, "NO." He refused to look up at her. Something warm crawled through the mitten on the hand with which he was holding himself up from the ice. It was blood. He was bleeding. He mashed his mittened hand to his nose. The blood guttered, his whole mitten went red.

Somebody swooped over him, scooped him up, lifted him to his feet. It was Mother. "Oh, Moonta," she said, "I was watching you; you were doing so well behind your chair, then you had to go and show off. Look at you!" She was angry because she was worried. She skated away with him, holding him, half lifting him. She hoisted him up to Aunt Cora. She tossed his chair up after him. Now Aunt Cora held him and started stooping over him in front of all the people on the ice.

Aunt Cora was worried too. "Ice is supposed to stop a nose bleed, not give you one," she joked nervously. She ripped the white scarf off her head, bundled it, and stuffed it under his nose. In no time the white scarf was a red mess.

Moonta was angry, and if the scarf hadn't been practically rammed into his mouth he would have yelled out at Aunt Cora, "You should talk—Father said you were always smash-

147

ing yourself bloody-nosed." He didn't say it. When he opened his mouth blood ran into it from under the scarf.

He saw all the people standing looking up at him. Mother was crouched, taking her skates off. The next moment the canal swam before Moonta's eyes. The whole canal blackened and seemed full of queer, mixed-up, blotchy, ballooning figures.

"I'm sick," he gasped from under the scarf to Aunt Cora. "I feel queer. I'm cold, but I'm sweating, and my knees are shaking."

"Don't talk," Aunt Cora ordered. "Swallowing blood will only make you sicker."

"Mother, I'm sick," Moonta said miserably as he saw his mother come scrambling up the bank.

But Aunt Cora laughed now. "Don't be scared, Moonta, you're not bleeding to death. What you've got is gape-hunger. Bet you couldn't eat any breakfast this morning, and the cold and hard work on skates . . ."

"Thank goodness, if that's what it is," Mother said. Then she plumped herself down on Moonta's little chair. "Why, I'm sick myself. I've got the ice-hunger too. I must confess— like any school girl—I couldn't eat breakfast either."

Then Moonta remembered. "I've got the bread with cheese in my jacket pocket."

Mother reached over into Moonta's pocket and dug out the

newspaper-wrapped bread. Aunt Cora took the scarf away and studied Moonta's smeared face. "It's stopped," she said. "You're going to live. That is, if you two skate-crazy people will let me run to my house and quick fix you a lunch." She stooped to take off Moonta's skates.

Mother stuffed half a slice of black bread into her mouth; she reached up and stuffed the other half into Moonta's mouth. "Why, what time is it?" she demanded, over her mouthful.

"Almost noon," Aunt Cora said.

Mother shook her head unbelievingly. "My, good time goes fast. Sure, run ahead. We two starved skeletons will come rattling on after we eat this."

Almost together Moonta and Mother swallowed their huge mouthfuls of bread and cheese. Almost together they said "Ah."

"Doesn't that clear up the eyes and brighten things?" Mother asked, even as she stuffed her mouth full again.

"I can see straight again," Moonta exclaimed. "Mother, I thought I was dying."

"Well, now that you haven't," Mother said, getting up and picking up the little red chair, "what say you and I stagger home toward more food?"

It was amazing how flat-footed and stiff he walked, Moonta thought. His ankles were as stiff as wood. Without skates under his feet he put his feet down so flat and hard, he felt like an old, plodding plow horse. Mother walked exactly the same way. Why, they walked like two tired old stiff people— with rheumatism in both legs.

Mother laughed as they looked down on themselves. "Now you know how it feels to be an earthling again, after feeling almost like a flying eagle. Isn't it awful? You almost feel as if you were a seal trying to get ahead on your flippers."

Oh, that was funny what Mother had said. "Mother," Moonta asked, "how do I skate?"

"You've got good skating feet—good ankles, and a good stroke. You're going to be a good skater."

Moonta glowed. "Then can we leave the chair home after lunch?"

Mother shook her head. "No, you're too reckless. You want to go at it too fast. Still skate with the chair this afternoon. Don't worry, I'll watch, and the moment I think you're ready, I'll toss the chair up on one of the canal boats, and you can practice without it."

"Then are we going to the New Church's Pipe?"

"We'll see, we'll see—one thing at a time. If you could only get that through your head, you wouldn't be a bloody-nosed mess now. You're trying to do too much too fast."

"But you said we were going to the Pipe," Moonta yammered. "And now just because I've got a bloody nose, you're

150

all scared. . . . Would we have gone if I hadn't got a bloody nose?"

"It didn't help," Mother said shortly.

It seemed so outrageous that just a bloody nose might keep him from getting to the New Church's Pipe, Moonta thought up a barefaced lie. "I fell because I had a loose shoelace, and my skate cut through it," he said angrily. "I can skate, you saw me when old Siebren had my chair."

"Moonta!" Mother said, shocked. "You lie! Just because I was skating with those boys; you may not have known it, but I was keeping an eye on you all the time. I saw you cut through your shoelace and throw the piece away where somebody else could trip on it and crash down. You lied this morning about eating the bread, too. And just because you're dead set to get to that Pipe is not any excuse for lying like that. You watch it, lad; a lying mouth, more than a bloody nose, is exactly what may stop me from going with you to that New Church's Pipe."

When Mother said "lad," and when she talked as if she were reading it from the Bible, Moonta knew it was time to be quiet. Still, the next moment it seemed he had to start again, even though he changed the subject a little. "If we don't get to go to the Pipe, then this afternoon can I get in one of those long lines behind you?"

Mother laughed at him. "Behind me, or would you rather be

151

the lead after a couple of hours of beginning to learn to skate?"

"No, the last one," Moonta said promptly. "I'd like to be the tail-ender. He really gets whipped around. When he has to let go just from sheer speed at the end of a sweep, he flies like a bullet."

"Exactly," Mother said. "That's it exactly. There you go again always wanting what is the most dangerous and reckless."

"Oh, all right," he grouched, "then I won't. I'll just get in the middle of your line." They were at Aunt Cora's house. Moonta hobbled ahead to open the door for Mother—to make things right after his grouching. "Mother . . ." he began.

As she stepped into the hall Mother whirled on him. "Get in the middle," she said indignantly. "You'll get right behind that chair, and you'll stay there as long as I say so. And no more begging me for anything. Isn't there ever going to be an end? Moonta, why must you be such a whining baby with me, and such a roughneck outside?"

"I don't know," he said slowly. "I guess maybe it's because I've got to do everything right now while there's ice. Don't you think I want to be a champion too?"

"Well," Mother said. "I don't know . . . I've been wondering if tomorrow in church I shouldn't pray for a big thaw."

"No, Mother," Moonta said, horrified. "That's the whole

trouble—if a thaw comes too soon. Mother, won't you, please, pray the other way?"

Mother just looked at him. It was time to be still—way past time.

10

The Hard Hand

IT SEEMED to take Aunt Cora an awfully long time to get lunch ready—maybe because she was so big and her kitchen so small. She moved about heavily. Mother helped her a bit, and between times hunched down and rubbed Moonta's stiff ankles. He had no patience with it, although his ankles felt as if steel bands were clamped around them. Now that he wasn't sick-hungry anymore, Moonta couldn't wait to get back to the canal.

Aunt Cora was *so* slow. She moved about the kitchen like a ponderous hippopotamus; her big thighs kept bumping the

154

table. To make himself patient Moonta sat dreaming about the New Church's Pipe. It seemed as far away and as unearthly and mysterious as ever. But there wasn't much sense dreaming about it, when he wasn't going there anyway—and just because of a little bloody nose. Anyway, maybe it was just an old black, rusty pipe hammered into the ground. Moonta wouldn't believe it—not even if he wasn't going there. It would be silly to go skating far out the long canal toward a piece of pipe!

At last Aunt Cora set a big platter of sandwiches in the middle of the table. Then she sat down. "Hey," Mother said, "the headmaster certainly was fine this morning, wasn't he? I don't know of anybody that could have got you over being shy and stubborn and shamed the way he did. I certainly couldn't. That's why I took off fast with that line of boys. I knew a boy wouldn't want his mother to take him by the hand and teach him in public. But the headmaster did just right. I can't understand why you've been scared of him."

Moonta swallowed his first bite of sandwich. He tried to explain it to himself so he could tell mother how it was that the headmaster became a completely different man outside of school. Before Moonta could think it out, suddenly sunshine came through the window. It shone down on the table.

With his mouth full of food, he croaked out to Mother, "The sun. The sun's come out!"

She said, "Yes, it certainly has. And there's been another

change in the wind. The wind's been changing all morning, and soon it'll be blowing from over land. Wind with strong sunshine . . ." She shook her head.

He had so hoped she would say: "Don't worry, Moonta. The sun's just peeking out. It'll go away in a minute."

Mother turned to Aunt Cora, who sat there munching so you could hear it. "I'm getting worried about our two men on that Eleven-Towns Tour. You know men. Riemer will think he's such a good skater he can outspeed even crumbling ice. I've known him to keep going with water standing on top of the ice. But now with him dragging Father . . ."

Aunt Cora solemnly agreed while she reached for another sandwich. "Lees didn't like that wind shifting even early this morning, and since then the wind's kept going around to the warmer landside. And now sun . . . I promised Lees I'd help her so she could skate a couple of hours this afternoon. She was going to sneak off to skate tomorrow, but now she's afraid that by then there'll be no ice—just watery stuff. I said I'd help her. Told her we could better sneak some sewing done on the Sabbath, especially hand sewing. That makes no noise."

"Cora!" Mother was shocked at her older sister. "You a daughter of an elder in the church, and sewing on Sunday."

But Moonta burst out, "Don't say that about watery stuff. Aunt Cora—don't say that!"

"I know you don't like to hear it, Moonta," Aunt Cora said.

156

But one's got to tell the truth at all times, especially the
daughter of an elder. Otherwise it's a sin. I'll actually be glad
of some sewing this afternoon," she told Mother. "It'll keep
me from the canal. I promise myself I'm not going to look at
the skating, but before I know it, there I'm back on the canal
bank, feeling like an old cluck hen with all her ducklings
swimming."

Mother and Aunt Cora talked on and on. Moonta sat still.
He just couldn't swallow his last mouthful of food. Then
amazingly Aunt Cora said in the midst of all her talking: "Go
outside, Moonta, and spit it out. I know you can't swallow.

I'll wrap a couple of these sandwiches, then you trot off and skate. Learn today while you have the chance. Don't miss a minute."

Now it was quicker and easier to swallow the mouthful. Moonta jumped up and grabbed his jacket.

"He didn't eat this morning, either," Mother said. "And he really ought to rest awhile."

"Not today," Aunt Cora said firmly. "If he learns well today, then at least he can start out a skater next year. He can rest the rest of the year. You of all people ought to understand."

Mother smiled at her vehemence. "I'd be on my way myself but I'd best start a big kettle of pea soup and sausage. The men will need that when they get back from their tour— something hearty and hot. I'd been sort of figuring on you to help, Cora, but if you promised Lees . . ."

"Well, I'd hate to drag Lees's sewing through the pea soup," Aunt Cora said.

Aunt Cora not only had the sandwiches wrapped the moment Moonta had his jacket buttoned, but she dug into her apron pocket and brought out a small handful of halfpennies. "For the sweepers," she told Moonta. "I imagine you'll be striking out up the canal this afternoon; you won't be satisfied staying at the village end with the small fry and girls and women."

"Oh, I've got some pennies," Moonta said.

"Take them anyway. You'll need plenty—the sweepers will

be out in force. They're pretty hungry after four watery winters, and now if they think the ice is going . . ."

"Thank you, Aunt Cora," Moonta said hastily, and tucked the halfpennies in his pocket.

"And listen, if you run out of coins, and any of those sweepers throws a broom between your feet, scoop it up and carry it a good way along the canal. Make him walk to get his broom back. That's how it's done, I'm told. It's not their canal and not their ice. The county just lets them make a few winter pennies this way."

"Cora!" Mother said. "You needn't teach him any rough stuff, he knows too much as it is." She turned to Moonta. "Don't go far up the canal; don't go beyond the third bend at the farthest, because it's going to be awfully hard to see the open water holes with snow getting in your eyes."

"Snow?" Moonta asked numbly. He looked at the steamy window. Through one clear strip of glass near the edge he saw that the sun had gone away. Now there was snow. Huge, wet, warm-looking flakes clung to the steamy windowpanes.

"Snow," he said. "Snow."

"Yes," Aunt Cora said. "It looks like this day we're getting everything from crackling frost to sun and wet snow and thaw. Seven kinds of weather in one day, but that's life for you at the edge of the North Sea."

Moonta couldn't say anything. He grabbed up his skates, grabbed the red chair, and flung out of the door.

159

Out in the street things seemed much better. A wind blew cold against his cheeks. And the snow wasn't wet, the snow flakes had just melted on the steamy kitchen window. Moonta sighed with relief and raced to the canal.

On the canal Moonta saw Lees. He drove straight and hard at her behind his chair. She'd just promised him things this morning to make him feel good. She'd known all the time—she'd told Aunt Cora all different. . . . "You said there'd be ice even Sunday," he accused Lees as he swept up behind her.

"Oh, Moonta," Lees said in surprise. "Boy, you worry too much. The beginning of this week you worried about this being another open, watery winter. Now there's ice, and you worry about its going away. You're learning to skate. Can't you ever be satisfied?"

"Yes, but," Moonta argued, "Father, and then even Mother, promised that if the ice stayed good, they'd skate with me to the New Church's Pipe. And if the ice goes, I'll have to wait another whole year, and a year—that's a long time."

"An eternity of eternities," Lees agreed. "But who's to say? There are snow flurries, and in between there's sunshine, and the wind keeps shifting. With a shifting wind you can't tell— it can shift right back again, and by night the cold could fall down and make stronger ice than ever. Meanwhile, why don't you just skate. It's about all you can do, I guess. God is doing the other things. So don't look at me."

Golly, Lees had said that by night it might all change. Maybe there'd still be a chance to get to the New Church's Pipe. Now Moonta wondered how far it was. He fished in his mind for some roundabout way of finding out from Lees. "If Father hadn't gone with Grandpa on the tour, I'd have gone to the New Church's Pipe with him today," he told Lees. "And I'm just learning, so I guess it can't be far."

"I'm afraid they promised you too much," Lees said. "Your father and mother are such good skaters they'd think nothing of a little jaunt to the Pipe. But I can tell you that to a poor skater like me, it'd be almost a journey out of the world. I've never been there myself."

Moonta's heart sank like a stone in water. Now the New Church's Pipe seemed more mysteriously far out along the long canal than ever.

"Well, lay on," Lees said. "Let's try it a few strokes, but we're not going to the New Church's Pipe. And we'll keep an eye on your chair."

It wasn't easy to "lay on" with Lees. She was so stooped Moonta had to reach far out to grasp the clasped hands she held on her back. Why, she was so stooped he could look over her shoulders. They started out, but he was too close, and Lees's skating too unsure. In about twenty strokes Lees laughed and gave up. "No, that wasn't a good idea of mine— a poor skater just makes another poor skater. Go get your chair."

For a little while he skated beside Lees with his chair, but she was so slow he got impatient. He had to show off by skating fast out ahead, then swirling back to her, and around her in great circles. "Oh, you're too good for me," Lees panted. She turned back to the village end of the canal. "I'll just stay at the end, then they won't have to carry me so far if I break my bones. My, if I went as fast as you, they'd have to pick me up in a bag, I'd be so full of broken bones."

Moonta laughed exultantly. Then, just to show Lees, he set out boldly up the canal toward the first bend and the village bridge. When Lees stopped to watch him, he was brave and cocky enough to send his little chair flying out ahead of him. He took out after it as fast as he could and caught it again. There—just like that—he'd invented a new game. Soon he found that he could skate almost as fast as the chair slid. It was even better because when he skated too fast and had to start windmilling his arms to keep on his feet, the sliding chair had slowed enough so he could grab it and skate on without hitch or a fall.

When he turned to look back, Lees was still watching. Then came her faraway yell: "You're good, Moonta—very good. But don't overdo it and set out for the Pipe, or go on the Eleven-Towns Tour."

It made Moonta so pleasantly confused he didn't know what to yell back. He was glad Lees was far away; he was blushing so, his cheeks felt warm enough to melt the ice. Then, because Lees was still standing there looking, he waved grandly and went farther up the canal toward where he could see the village bridge looming up at the bend.

Before he went around the bend, Moonta looked back. Lees had skated away. It was lonely here. There wasn't anyone. He remembered the warning of open water under the bridges—maybe that was what was scaring people away from skating near the bridge. He skated on slowly, so that if Lees did look back it would look as if he were still skating on into unknown distances.

When Moonta looked back again, he was around the bend; the village end of the canal was out of sight. Man, the bridge that he often walked over looked high from down below—high and dark. A new flurry of thick snowflakes made the bridge loom still darker. The darkness under the bridge looked like open, black water. Then Moonta saw the ropes around the real water hole. There was only a narrow ice passageway between the ropes around the rim of the hole and the pier of the bridge.

Still there were skate scratches on the narrow ice path. In the fine glow of Lees's praise Moonta hated to give up and turn back. Oh, there was no snow under the bridge, that's why it looked so dark. If he turned around now, Lees couldn't see him—she wouldn't know how far he had gone up the canal. Moonta laughed a hollow laugh at himself. Here he'd been going to go all the way to the New Church's Pipe with Father or Mother, and now he was scared of the first water hole under the first bridge.

Suddenly he swooped under the bridge past the water hole, but he closed his eyes. When he opened them again, he was beyond the hole and coming from under the bridge. Why, the narrow strip of ice hadn't even bent under his weight—well, hardly any.

Beyond the bridge there was a short, straight stretch before the canal turned abruptly in another sharp bend. He'd skate to that bend and turn back, Moonta decided. Even while he decided he had misgivings. If there'd only been one other skater going or coming, but here there was no one. Mother had said not to go beyond the third bend, so it ought to be safe. Still, that had been at lunch time; maybe now it wasn't safe anymore. Otherwise there'd be people. Little prickles

164

of horror went up Moonta's legs. Without deciding it, he whipped around and raced back to the bridge.

When he skated out from under the bridge again, it was snowing. In the short snow flurry a man had come onto the ice and was sweeping a clean path in the middle of the canal. The man had just started, but Moonta went down the swept path, grabbling for one of the halfpennies Aunt Cora had given him. With his mittened hand he couldn't get hold of one of the small coins, and the path was so short Moonta was over it before he realized.

There was a swish and dry rattle behind him. The sweeper had sent the broom spinning and swishing flat over the ice. The brush end of the broom shot between Moonta's feet, tripped him, flung him forward. His chair crashed down, and Moonta tumbled headlong over it. There was a sharp, crackling sound. Moonta had landed so hard on the chair its seat had split down the middle.

He painfully picked himself up, slowly set his chair up. But when he stood straight on his feet, a sharp pain shot from his knee to his ankle. It sickened him. Stooped over the chair, he tenderly rubbed his ankle; he clenched his teeth with the pain. Then to his relief it wasn't the ankle at all; it was his knee. He prodded at the knee with his mittened thumb. Then the sweeper was there. Through tear pains Moonta blinked up at the man.

"Twist your ankle?" the man said in a hard voice. "Didn't

break anything?" Then he raged. "That's it with you kids. Let a man sweep himself to death, and think you're smart if you can speed by without paying for the clean ice you used. Serves you right—had it coming."

"I didn't see you in time, the snow was in my eyes," Moonta said woefully. "And when I did, I couldn't get my halfpenny so quick."

"Sure," the man said, "that's the way it was—it always is, if I catch you. You bigger kids do it every year."

"I didn't. I can't even skate. Why do you suppose I have to skate with a chair?"

The man stooped down to rub Moonta's ankle. Moonta jerked angrily away. "It's my knee, not my ankle, but it isn't your fault it isn't my ankle." Then Moonta looked at the man's hard face with its stubble of black beard and was scared. He hastily fished out a halfpenny. But when he handed it over, he accidentally dropped the small coin.

The big man got down on his hands and knees and scrabbled for the coin in the snow. Even though his knee pained fiercely, it made Moonta feel miserable to see it. It must be awful to be so poor that a big, tough-faced man had to go down on his knees and scratch for a halfpenny.

The man found the coin. "How's your knee?" he asked.

"Getting much better," Moonta said wanly. "I guess I just hurt my crazy bone."

166

"That's in your elbow, kid," the man joked. "Unless you're crazy all over."

Moonta didn't laugh. "You broke my chair—the seat's split in two."

Still kneeling where he was, the man grabbed the chair, and he was so strong he just took it in one hand and squeezed the little seat together against the muscle of his arm. He fished in his pocket, took out a short length of twine, wound it around the seat, and knotted it. "That should do it. If not, you'll have two half chairs—one for each foot so you can skate in two directions at once."

Now the sweeper was poking fun, and suddenly angry, Moonta thought of what Aunt Cora had told him. As he thought of it he did it. He scooped up the broom, threw it across the chair, and raced away from the kneeling man.

Then Moonta was scared—as scared as he'd ever been in his life. It turned out he wasn't half the skater he thought he was—not even behind his chair. Hard as he raced, the man, who had jumped to his feet and was chasing him, was catching up—and he didn't have skates. Moonta ripped off his mitten, grabbed a halfpenny, and dropped it; but he dropped his mitten with it. He didn't look back.

The sweeper must have seen him drop the coin on the ice. He stooped, picked it up on the run, and came on again.

167

"Back here with that broom," he yelled hoarsely. "Bring that broom back, you miserable thieving pup . . . Hey, you dropped your mitten."

On he pounded after Moonta over the slippery ice. Just then the broom tipped off the chair and fell on the ice. Moonta sucked in his breath in his relief. But the sweeper let the broom lie, came on hard. Now Moonta raced as he had never raced in his life. The split chair screaked and squealed as the two pieces of seat jiggled and rubbed against each other. Suddenly the sweeper stopped, sent a stream of curses after Moonta, and went back for his broom.

Moonta raced on. His breath sobbed out, but still he didn't dare to slow down. At last he looked back. He couldn't even see the man in the thick snow that fell. Gradually Moonta slowed. The snow fell harder; Moonta held his head down to keep the snow out of his eyes and skated on behind the squiggling, creaky chair.

The next moment he gasped out in terror. Something grabbed him from behind. In the soft snowfall the sweeper had stolen up and grabbed him. He jerked Moonta off the ice. "Glad you furnished the chair," he gritted out. He planted one big wooden-shoe foot on the seat of the chair, hoisted Moonta up over his knee.

"But I gave you a whole penny," Moonta yammered.

"Yes, and now I'm going to give you what you should have had long ago. So you gave me a penny; your folks ought to give me a guilder for doing their work for them. How'd they ever let you grow up this way?"

With the man's foot planted on the chair, only the chair seat squealed as he whaled away with his hard hand. Moonta didn't let out a whimper, he held himself deathly still. After his scare, bad as this was, this was nothing— Anyway he wasn't going to cry— not one sound.

At last the hard-breathing man set him down. Moonta straightened out slowly, both hands on the seat of his pants. How he managed it he didn't know, but suddenly he could even make a small joke. "Now I've *got* to skate," he told the grim man. "I'm sure as the dickens not going to sit down."

It made the man smile; one slight corner of his mouth twisted. Suddenly he stuck out his hand. Moonta had to shake it. "Are we friends now?" the sweeper said. "You've got better stuff in you than I thought you had."

169

"If I did, you knocked it all out," Moonta said bitterly.

"Well, are we friends? Then I'll promise not to toss any more brooms, if you'll promise not to be so fresh."

Moonta nodded, then abruptly skated away. If he was going to cry he was going to do it alone—but he wasn't going to.

As he skated slowly and stiffly along Moonta thought darkly of Aunt Cora. She'd told him to do it. Boy, was he going to tell her off! He shook his head. No. How she would laugh! Her whole big body would shake and jiggle.

Again Moonta became aware there was somebody following him. For a moment his heart closed, so sure he was that it was the sweeper again. He didn't dare look back; he scampered ahead, raced hard toward the people at the end of the canal.

There was a laugh. It was Mother! She was skating right tight behind him, watching his every skate stroke. "Mother," he yelped out. Then in his relief he had to show off. "Mother," he yelled, "watch!" He sent his chair flying, raced after it so fast that he passed it, and skirled in a fine bird swoop around it, making a swirl of ice scrapings and flying snow. He grabbed the chair again, sent it flying straight at Mother, chased after the chair and toward her as fast as his feet would fly.

Mother grinned and nodded her approval. She grabbed up the chair and held it high above her head. "Broke it, didn't you? Well, you don't need it anymore. Come along, proud lad,

we'll set this red thing on the deck of the first canal boat."
She skated away, the chair held high.

For a moment Moonta stood stock-still in shocked surprise.
Then he let out a yelp, and chased after Mother. He caught
up, skated like a man right beside his mother. Once he even
tried to clasp his hands on his back the way the older men did,
but then he found he had to wiggle-waggle and twist his
shoulders.

"No," Mother said. "You're a boy, you can still swing your
arms for balance—get that balance first. That's the next lesson.
You've got your skating feet—good sturdy skating legs, good
ankles—all you need now is to be sure that both in your mind
and in your feet you're a good skater. You mustn't have the
chair anymore now, Moonta; you'll get to depend on it. Now
you've got to become sure of yourself—know you're not going
to fall. You never will be, if there's always something to catch
on to."

They drove straight up to the first canal boat lying in a row
of seven boats against the dike side of the canal. The boat
had a name, *The Six Brothers,* painted on it in white lettering.
Mother swept alongside, reached up, and tossed the chair on
the deck. "I've put a little chair on your deck," she called out
to a window with three pots of geraniums in its sill. "Is it all
right? We'll pick it up before dark."

A voice answered something from inside the boat, and
Mother skated away with Moonta beside her. It was the

171

biggest moment of his whole life. There stood the little red chair in the snow, redder than the three geraniums. He skated with Mother, and even though he knew she was holding down her speed, it still was the proudest moment of his life. Moonta was so proud, he then and there asked Mother right out: "Now shall we go to the New Church's Pipe?" Mother didn't seem to have noticed his stiff, sore knee. And in the thick, short snowfall she evidently hadn't seen him get his terrible spanking. Moonta decided he wasn't going to mention a thing—it might spoil any chance for a trip to the Pipe.

His high hopes were dashed the next moment. "I wish your father and grandpa were home," Mother said with a quick look up in the sky. "That's why I'm here skating. I decided that instead of making pea soup, I'd first get in some skating while the ice was still good. Oh, I wish those two were home. The snow's making it difficult to see, and I hear there are water holes falling into the ice wherever there are draught ditches emptying into the canal. They can't rope them off fast enough. That's a bad sign. It's a real sign of a change in the weather. Ice knows it first."

Mother didn't say—she didn't have to—that there wasn't the slightest chance now of going to the Pipe. Instead she said, "Well, I'd better be getting back to my pea soup. I've got the peas soaking. But you know how it is with good times on ice—like this morning, I'm sure it's much later than we think." She looked at Moonta worriedly. "Don't go up the canal again, will you? Not too far, and not alone. You haven't got the chair to help you now, if you should skate blind into a water hole. Promise me?"

Moonta nodded his head.

"Well," Mother said again, reluctantly, "I suppose I'd better get going. I surely want to have a hearty, warm meal all ready when the men come. But I wouldn't be surprised if they have to come walking the last miles of the way. So promise me after I'm gone, you won't go far up the canal. You won't, will you?"

"No," Moonta said. But he made it the smallest 'no' he knew how to make.

Mother skated away.

11

The Six Brothers

FOR A long time Moonta skated up and down in the area of the seven canal boats. It was always nice to turn back to *The Six Brothers* and look at the little red chair on the tarry-looking old canal boat. It stuck out like a sore, red thumb. Moonta thought everybody must see it. Everybody but Lees, of course. She came stooping by all alone, because she was such an awkward skater nobody, not even the older women, wanted her in their line.

Moonta waited for Lees near the prow of *The Six Brothers*. He wanted Lees to see the chair on the deck of the boat. Lees came clawing by—it was lucky she was so near the ice, for stooped as she was she always seemed to be falling.

Lees did not see Moonta, let alone see the red chair. "Hey, Lees, how about it?" he yelled mannishly. "Lay on, lay on."

Lees straightened and blinked and then saw it was Moonta. "Oh, Moonta," she said. "But 'lay on'—not on your life. We almost went down in a heap once before."

"No, but, Lees," he said importantly, "this time I'll lead."

As he said it he came in a skirling, graceful swirl around her, although he did have to spread his arms quite a bit away from his body to keep his balance. Lees stood astounded. "But, Moonta, where is your chair?"

Proudly Moonta pointed up to the deck of the boat. Snow was covering the seat, hiding the crack, but the back of the chair and all its rungs stood out redder than ever in the white snow. "My land, my land!" Lees exclaimed. "There it stands, and there you stand free on skates. And to learn in such a short time."

Standing there sure and straight and proud on his skates, he felt sorry for Lees. "Come on, lay on—we'll go all the way to the bridge with me in the lead," he urged.

"Well," Lees said doubtfully. "I really should be getting home. I can't let your poor Aunt Cora do all my sewing. . . ." Lees fished a small watch on the end of a black shoestring-like cord, from somewhere down in her clothes, peered at it through the snowflakes, and wiped it off. "My land, my land—

it's four o'clock, Moonta. Four o'clock. I've got to go back. So I'll 'lay on'—but don't you go too fast or too wild, hear. Otherwise you'll be dragging me on my back behind you like a sack of potatoes." Moonta was proud that Lees thought he could go that wild and fast. Imagine, and only minutes ago he'd still been using the little red chair.

He looked up at the chair on the deck. "Four o'clock," he said. "Maybe, Lees, if Father should get back early he'd still go with me to the New Church's Pipe."

Lees shook her head. "I don't want to disappoint you, the way you've got your heart set on that trip, but now look. I haven't told anybody—and nobody has noticed it with the snow in their eyes—but look!" She pulled him over and pointed to the bottom of *The Six Brothers*. "See that edge of water? See that boat lying free? The ice has melted away from it all around. That's the surest sign the ice is going, and going fast. Unless the wind changes in the night, I'm afraid that by tomorrow these boats will be pushing their way up the canal again, the ice will be so rotten and crumbly. And then no more skating until the next freeze. But don't tell anybody; let them have fun while it lasts."

Moonta stared forlornly at the small rim of water edging the hull of *The Six Brothers*. He started when Lees touched him. He hastily put his clasped hands on the small of his back, and Lees laid her small claw of a hand in them. Then he was proud, for while it went slow and while he had to wiggle-

176

waggle his shoulders too much, they didn't go down. They skated neatly, without a stumble or a hitch or a halt. Then Lees dug the heels of her skates into the ice and they scraped to a halt. "I've got to go now," she said. "But all I can say is that you are a one-day wonder. Such skating, even with me in tow. Why, hardly anybody but your father and mother can have me behind them and not go down on their faces. Boy, you are a true son of your father and mother."

Moonta blushed so hard in his delight, he had to skate hastily away. He even stumbled a little, but Lees wasn't looking; she was stooped over, taking off her skates. "Bye, Lees," he called.

In his pride Moonta almost skated full tilt into the headmaster. The headmaster windmilled his arms and spread his legs wide to come to a halt. Moonta sailed around him, head straight up, then came to a graceful, ice-scraping stop.

The headmaster had snow stuck to his eyebrows. He dashed it away. "Moonta, my eyes don't deceive me? Aren't you the boy with the chair? But I don't see anything red—just a steely flash of flying skates."

"It is I," Moonta remembered to say properly as if he were in school.

"Well, then may I borrow your chair?" the master joked.

Moonta pointed across the canal to the *The Six Brothers*. "See it? We'll go get your chair."

"Oh, now, Moonta, it was a sort of joke. Still, seriously, if you learned that well, and my old pride would allow it—a good chair wouldn't be a bad idea. One with a high back—say the minister's chair off the pulpit."

Then, without any word of objection, the master got behind Moonta. It was hard getting under way, then when they had their pace matched, the headmaster pushed too hard. Moonta leaned forward, but the push of the master's hand against the small of his back straightened him out, even made him skate stomach forward. He was skating almost on his heels. In a moment they'd go down like silly fools.

"Hey, you're pushing," Moonta shouted. "You shouldn't push, you're not the lead. . . . " He gasped as he said it. He was shouting right out at the headmaster. "I just learned, I haven't got speed yet," he hastily added.

To his immense relief the headmaster laughed. "You're right, I was, and I shouldn't." Now the headmaster held back, and then in the next few strokes they swung into the smooth, swaying, effortless rhythm they needed. They went like the wind, the snow blew against Moonta's cheeks, and he laughed out in joy. Behind him the master kept encouraging, kept muttering, "Good boy, good boy—and all this in one day."

Just then three of the big sixth graders bore down on them and skirled to a stop. "Hey, look, fellows, it's Moonta, and he's got the headmaster in tow. What do you know, what do you know?"

Moonta went warm with pride, even though his knee hurt from the strain of pulling the headmaster along. For a moment he didn't know anything to say that wouldn't sound cocky to the master and the big boys. But he didn't have to think up anything—the three boys were so full of themselves and their big deeds, they were babbling and babbling to the master. "We've been all the way to Ternaard," they told him. "In almost no time. We'd have done it in record time, except that on the way back all kinds of holes had fallen into the ice. We still made some of the bridges, but it's open water under almost all of them, and the ice is going fast. We're glad we're back. They're not bothering to rope off the holes anymore."

The master shook and shook his head, and made little concerned sounds with his lips.

"Well, we did it, but we're sure glad we're back. It's pesky when you have to take your skates off and run around the bridges. Well, guess this is the end of our holiday, isn't it, Master? School again Monday. Grrrr."

"Grrrr is right," the master said. "And if you think I prefer school to ice—well, I can just tell you that the ice is no harder than your heads."

The three boys, hot, red, and steamy, skated away laughing. . . . "Well, Moonta," the headmaster said, "shall we race?"

But Moonta wasn't eager. The sixth graders had spoiled everything with their awful news. Now it was sure he wouldn't get to the New Church's Pipe this winter—unless ice came

179

again. But it seldom did. "If it's as bad as they said," he told the master, "then my father and grandfather will have to walk back from their Eleven-Towns Tour."

"Oh, don't take it too literally, Moonta. They just wanted to feel like heroes. It isn't as bad as all that. Just always remember that everybody exaggerates to make a good story. It makes him a tall hero inside his tall tale. . . . Come on, race you to the other side of the canal."

They raced, but not in the way they had intended. Across the canal where the boats lumped dark in the falling snow there were sudden loud voices—arguing, quarreling voices.

"A fight," the headmaster said. "Come on, Moonta, never miss a good fight or a good fire."

When Moonta and the headmaster neared the boats, it looked almost as if the whole village had gathered around *The Six Brothers*. A short, fat woman stood on the deck of the boat. Arms dug in her sides, she was defiantly yelling back to the massed skaters. "And I tell you, we're going to move," she screamed. "We're pushing off. Your rotten ice is melting, and if you had one grain of sense, you'd know you're not going to be skating anymore by nightfall. Look at the water around our boat—a foot of it—we're lying clear. All that ice needs is some pushing."

"A foot—*my* foot," a woman in the crowd yelled back at her. "There isn't three inches of water around your stinking scow."

"Stinking scow, eh? Well, we're selling petroleum, not perfume," the wrathful woman shot back at her. "If your ladyship can't stand the smell, get off the ice. Bet you haven't even got your beds made yet—playing on the ice all day. That's what's wrong with this village—you people are all skate crazy. See the name of this boat, it's *The Six Brothers*, and soon it'll be *The Seven Brothers*, and I can't feed my six boys ice. All this time we haven't made a guilder here. You're so ice crazy you don't even eat or go home, and you sure don't buy petroleum. For all of you, we can starve here."

"Then what makes you so fat—and so ugly?" somebody shouted up.

"Ugly, eh?" the woman spat. "Well, don't worry, I'll get out of your sight. I'm going to the helm, and my husband and three of my kids are getting their pushing poles—we're pushing off. Whether we break up your ice, or the weather and God do it—what's the difference? This way we can still make it to the next village before Sunday, and maybe sell a gallon

181

or two of oil. We'll starve to death here at this dead end of the canal."

She turned and strode fiercely to the helm. As she passed the hatch she yelled down, "Are you coming up with the push poles or not? Let's get going. And I don't care if this whole miserable village goes down in the water when we break the ice—with their skates on!"

The crowd surged forward. "And we're telling you," a man shouted, "that if you break up our ice, you needn't come back here again—in all eternity."

"That'd be too soon," the woman screamed back.

Now the husband, a big man, twice as tall as his broad wife, came up with the push poles. Three scrawny boys followed him. "Look," the big skipper said mildly down to the muttering crowd, "it's really as she says. Six hungry boys to feed; we can't just lie here. We've got to get going."

"But, friend," the headmaster asked, "isn't it doubtful—you've got to break ice all the way—that you can make it to the next village and still sell petroleum before Sunday?"

"Don't listen to that smooth, barefaced talker," the woman yelled from the tiller. "Why should we do something for them? They haven't done anything for us. Are you going to stand there, or do we shove off?"

The crowd closed in, talking and threatening. A man at the head of the mob yelled up, "Give that boat one push, and we'll rip it to pieces with our bare hands."

"Looks like we're not going to have to push it," the woman at the helm suddenly cackled in a horrible, gap-toothed laugh. "Just look at the ice sinking under you from all your weight." She jeered when the crowd made a sudden wild retreat as the water pressed up from the open rim around the boat and welled out over the ice.

Away from the boat the people massed again, even surged forward as far as they thought it safe. But now the headmaster was in the front row. Moonta squirmed through the crowd to be with him. "Look, all we ask is an hour or two more," the headmaster said. "We know you've got your living to make, but by then it'll be dark and we'll be going home."

"Oh, the smooth talker again," the woman snarled. "Come back here and push with that pole," she ordered her husband.

He stood doubtful.

"No," the headmaster said to the man. "Instead, put your wooden shoe on the end of your push pole and hand them both down to me. We can do this in a way so that nobody suffers."

The woman came running from the tiller. "Can't you see it's a trick, so they get our poles and we can't push off?" she raged at her husband. She was so blind with rage she didn't see Moonta's red chair. She stumbled over it. The whole crowd hooted at her. The woman grabbed up the chair. "And who gave any of you permission to throw your junk on our deck?"

"You did!" Moonta, next to the master, yelled out in indignation. "I heard you myself. My mother asked, and you said it was all right."

"Why, you whey-faced pipsqueak, yelling back at me! I'll give you your chair." The woman snapped the cord, ripped the whole chair in two where the seat was cracked, and flung it at Moonta. "There's your chair. Now you've got two."

Moonta flung up his hands and managed to catch one section. The headmaster caught and pulled down the other piece before it could hit Moonta in the face.

The master laid a warning hand on Moonta's trembling arm. He ignored the yelling fishwife. Instead he said up to the skipper, "I asked you to hand down your pole and one wooden shoe. We'll make it right, so we'll have our ice, and your six boys won't go hungry."

The woman tried to stop her husband as the master skated up to the boat and the black, welling water. The skipper turned on her. "Get down that hatch and stop your big mouth," he said angrily. "Stuff a feather bed in it if you have to. Why must you always get us into trouble? Can't you see these people mean well?"

The muttering woman slowly turned, slowly walked toward the hatch. Now the skipper of *The Six Brothers* turned to the master and handed down push pole and shoe. "We don't take alms," he said quietly.

"Well, I'm going to," the headmaster said. "Meanwhile,

184

you can roll a barrel of petroleum to the bank, and I'll person-
ally make up whatever we're short."

"First toss up that split chair," the skipper said. "I'll fix it."

Moonta skated up to the boat with the two sections of
chair. He reached up as high as he could, the big skipper
leaned down, but suddenly the whole chair fell apart—
spindles and rungs rained down on Moonta, bounced off his
head and shoulders. The whole crowd chuckled and laughed.
"Better have him make a bird cage of it now," someone
yelled. Moonta fumed.

Then, as Moonta stooped and grabbed the pieces of chair
together, the headmaster suddenly thrust the big wooden
shoe hanging over the knob at the end of the push pole before
Moonta's face. "Might as well start the collection with you,
if you're not too busy." The master laughed.

Moonta reared up, straightened, suddenly spat into the
shoe dangling before his face. He hadn't intended to do it,
he'd just done it. He hastily reached out to wipe out the shoe
with his mittened hand, but the headmaster skated up to him.
"Did you admire that fishwife on the deck?" he asked very
softly.

Moonta dumbly shook his head.

"Do you admire yourself now that you're acting like her?"
the master whispered insistently. Moonta had nothing to say.

"For that little performance," the headmaster said in a low,

185

hard voice, "you'll do a thousand lines after school on Monday, and you'll write: 'I'm a poor peacemaker, slow to forgive, so I'll always be in trouble.'"

"But she threw my chair off the boat, and now look at it," Moonta said. "And . . ."

"No *and's* and no *but's*. One thousand lines," the master said. "And eight halfpennies or four pennies from you." Moonta tore off his wet mitten, and sullenly dropped the eight coins. Behind him three big girls snickered and giggled.

As the master skated away with his collection shoe on the end of the pole Moonta heard him say to the first group of grown people, "After this collection hadn't we big folks better get off the ice with all our weight, and let the children have this last hour? Not you, Moonta," he called over his shoulder. "As soon as the skipper gives back your chair, you're to get off the canal."

Moonta acted as if he didn't hear, but he looked all around for his mother. She didn't seem to be here, at least she wasn't saying one word to help him out. He desperately hoped she was still home making pea soup.

It wasn't the master's canal, it wasn't his ice. Anyway, Moonta wrathfully told himself, he didn't care. The ice was going, it'd soon be all over. But even if there was ice, he'd have to write the lines all day Monday. He knew only too well when his parents heard of this, they'd add their punishment; and even if there was no school on Monday they'd make him write the thousand lines on the kitchen table at home. They always backed up the teachers—never him. He was always in the wrong. Always.

The skipper on deck was suddenly talking to him and handing down the little red chair. "I fixed it the best I could, boy. It's all together again, and I nailed two cleats under the split seat. . . . And I didn't spit on it."

Everybody laughed and went on laughing. Suddenly, so fiercely rebellious that he wanted to bawl out at them, Moonta slammed his chair down on the ice. Now even the fishwife had come back up and was standing smiling beside her husband. But it was the headmaster she smiled at as he came back with the wooden shoe full of coins. "I called you barefaced, and I called you smooth," the woman said. "Well, you are smooth, and you've smoothed me out. So I think we'll be back in a few weeks with *The Seven Brothers.*"

"Couldn't you make it *The Six Brothers and Sister?*" the schoolmaster asked. "It'd take a little more paint, but wouldn't it be fine?"

The woman beamed. "I'll see what I can do for you, Master."

Moonta raged. Now they were silly and sickening. The master was busy handing up the coin-filled wooden shoe. Fiercely Moonta turned and dove in among the groups of people behind his chair. He had to be away. And he didn't care; he wasn't going to get off the canal. He'd make it look as if he were going for the opposite bank, but once away from the crowd and the headmaster, and curtained from sight by falling snow, he'd swing around and streak away toward the bend and the bridge.

He was sullenly scared at what he was doing, but even so, he couldn't help noticing that he was skating really fast on behind the sturdy, fixed chair. Couldn't he—couldn't he with the chair skate by himself to the New Church's Pipe? He wouldn't get nearly so tired with the chair, and he'd be going three—five times faster. He was going to be punished anyway for spitting in the shoe. They'd never go with him now to the Pipe, if he knew anything—not even if the ice stayed. And now the snow was slowing, it was stopping at last. Oh, it was a fine idea to have thought of going with the chair. Father always said that if you skated fast enough you could usually get over the thinnest ice. It might cave down behind you, but you'd be over, and racing on.

As Moonta neared the bridge he looked back. It didn't look as if anybody had seen him going up the canal. Anyway, seeing him with a chair nobody would think he was going far. Moonta skated on again. He came by the spot where the sweeper had given him his terrible spanking. For a moment it gave him pause. The sweeper was gone. . . . Anyway, he told

188

himself, he was only trying it out around the next bend or two—most likely he couldn't get anywhere near the New Church's Pipe. But it was his last chance even to try. And the only way he could stay on the canal.

This time Moonta boldly swept on under the dark village bridge.

12

The Pipe

MOONTA and the chair swept around the third bend in the canal, far beyond the village bridge. This was the farthest he had been. It was new territory, and it looked strange and sort of lonely. But the snow had stopped. He could look far ahead now. Still, except for the hole under the village bridge, there hadn't been a water hole anywhere so far. Anyway, with snow on the rest of the canal, any water hole would show up as black as soot and sin.

Why, it was just as Father had said the other day—away from the dike and the sea, as the canal went inland the ice

was much better than between their village and its bridge.
Those three big kids from the sixth grade had said it was
awful out here. Of course the master had told him they'd
just made tall tales to make themselves big, tall heroes. . . .
The school teacher certainly knew an awful lot of things.
He'd even known how to handle the horrible fishwife on
The Six Brothers. But he'd ordered him to write one thousand
lines and he hadn't even been in school. The headmaster had
been friendly and full of fun all day, yelling at everybody,
but he'd ordered him off the canal. It wasn't fair!

Anyway, the ice was good here, and the snow had stopped.
The clouds hung low in the west, so the sun didn't come out—
everything was getting much better than it had been. Of
course here the wind was blowing differently, but that wasn't
because the wind had changed; it was because the canal had
turned inland. And Lees had told him that if the wind stayed
in one place and stopped shifting, then by night it might
turn biting cold again—freeze so hard you could hear it
crackle.

Now far beyond the third bend, right up ahead, black poles
and brown rope rose up from the ice. That spelled a water
hole. It must be that a draught ditch with its current drained
into the canal there. But the canal was widening, and Moonta
steered a course to the edge of the canal as far away from the
roped black water hole as possible.

The snow had blown up against the canal bank; he couldn't

191

see the cracks in the ice. One leg of his chair caught in the deep, unseen crack. Moonta lifted the chair just in time, or he would have gone buckling over it. On flying skates he hopped the unseen crack. Hey, he'd jumped clear off the ice with the chair held up and he'd just skated on without a hitch or a stumble. He hadn't done that before.

Now the canal was one straight stretch. Far up ahead Moonta saw a dark figure skating in the same direction he was going. It must be an old man, he rode so stately straight, and his long endless strokes carried him almost from one side of the canal to the other. It was the old-fashioned way of skating. Father had often told him that that way you went more sideways than ahead, but it looked important. If an old man skated here, that spelled safe ice. Glad to see a human, Moonta raced after the old man.

Then Moonta looked back. Behind him a slim woman's figure was coming around the bend. It must be Mother after him. Was it Mother? Moonta raced madly, sure it must be his mother. Someone had seen him skating away from the crowd at *The Six Brothers* and had told her.

It was no use scurrying and scuttling and racing. Mother could catch up with him in easy strokes. But he had to race on—Boy, would she be mad! And if they'd told her about him spitting in the wooden shoe and having to do one thousand lines for the master . . . He raced on in anguish. At last he dared look back. The woman skater—whoever she was—

wasn't Mother, because now she'd turned and was skating back.

Moonta bent over the chair, leaned on it hard in his sagging relief. That way he passed the old man. Behind him the man called out, "Still got to get to Amsterdam by night?"

Moonta laughed. "No, Rotterdam. Then over the river and up. I'm from Switzerland."

After the big scare that the woman had been Mother, it was good to joke. But the old man grumped. "Smart kids, nowadays."

Soon he was far behind Moonta. There was another bend. Around the bend was the longest sweep of straight canal Moonta had yet seen. There were sweepers on the straight stretch, and even a tent. He could see the piles of oranges on its counter. The orange of the little pyramid was such a sudden color in all the whiteness it leaped out at him. It was so tempting he veered toward the white tent.

But the scare of the woman skater he'd thought was Mother lay deep in him. He told himself Mother could still easily catch up with him and haul him back. He grabbled for coins; he mustn't get a broom tossed between his feet again. It reminded him that his knee still hurt. If Mother found out that besides everything else he'd gone off with a sore knee . . . oh, boy, would he get it!

He must be going mighty fast, for now he was on the smooth-swept streak in the middle of the canal—almost before

193

he knew it. He tossed a coin at the first sweeper. "Any water holes up ahead?" he yelled like an old experienced skater.

"Yes, under the next bridge, but you can sail over it in your chair; just use your hands for paddles," the sweeper joked as he ran after the halfpenny. There was another sweeper, and farther on, still a third. But there were very few people skating.

"Where's everybody?" he called out to the third sweeper as he dropped his penny.

"Gone home to supper like decent people," the man yelled back. "They'll be out in the evening again. It's moonlight, you know."

Moonta hadn't thought of that! Why, the moon would be up early. Of course, it rose an hour later every night. What time had it been that the moon came up last night when he'd lain dreaming about the New Church's Pipe? Moonta couldn't think. Imagine, it could easily be that he'd see the New Church's Pipe by moonlight. There it'd stand tall, dark and looming, far out this long, long canal, and the moon would be rising behind it. Just the same, he'd take one quick look, and then whip around and streak for home. But the moon would be out and light his way back.

Imagine skating by moonlight. Imagine having gone all the way to the New Church's Pipe all alone his very first day of skating. It would be worth the thousand lines about being a peacemaker; it'd be worth any punishment. Why, if the ice

194

didn't stay, there'd be the whole dreary winter, and you might as well sit in school after school and write lines. There'd be nothing else to do.

There were fewer and fewer people on the ice because there was no village near, just farms. The farmers must have gone home to milk their cows. Much later Moonta passed a small hamlet, and the sign at the edge of the canal read SEVEN HOUSES. That sign no doubt must be for the skippers of the canal boats. Seven Houses. Why, he'd never even come this far by road. Just once he remembered seeing the glint of the sun on the roofs of Seven Houses from far away across many flat fields. And now he was riding past Seven Houses, except there were nine—Moonta counted them as he raced past.

Here at the hamlet there were people again, just a little cluster, skating up and down and having fun. But they made a gabble of noise. The yells and laughter sounded so good after so much loneness, he waved at them all as he sped by

One woman stopped and waved back. "Where are you from, and where are you going so late in the day?"

Moonta just waved with one hand, but didn't slow down and didn't answer. Behind him he heard the woman say, "Somebody ought to stop that boy. He's still skating with a chair. He's not from anywhere around here, but he keeps going up the canal. It's crazy. Does he know where he's going?"

Over his shoulder Moonta yelled out, "Sure. Amsterdam."

They all laughed, and he skated on around a new bend in the canal. Around the bend everything was lonely and quiet again, and now he wished he hadn't been so smart. It would have been better if he'd asked how far it still was to the New Church's Pipe. Ahead in the middle of the canal, as if the ice had closed around it in its sailing, lay a canal boat. He would ask somebody there. But the boat lay high, lone, and dark. There was nobody around. There were no lights in the windows. It was sort of scary, as if the lone boat had been abandoned, and there was nothing for miles around. Moonta gave it a wide berth. Still, as he looked anxiously out of the corners of his eyes, he could not deny that around this boat, too, stood a narrow ribbon of water. It was almost as wide as the strip of water had been around *The Six Brothers*.

The dark hull of the boat made him anxious. It even felt as if the ice under him were bowing and yielding a little from his weight. Of course it was all imagination. When he was alone and a little scared and worried, there'd come a small lump in his stomach. And then his knee began to hurt. It was as if his conscience were in his knee, Moonta thought to himself for a little joke. He looked back, almost hoping he would see a swift skater overtaking him—almost wanting Mother to haul him back. There was no one. He thought of turning back, but shook his head stubbornly. Now if he went back, and had done nothing and got nowhere, it would all be foolish and he'd get punished just the same.

As Moonta rounded the next bend he was glad to see another tent. It was much better to skate toward than to a lonely, tarry, black boat. On sudden impulse he scraped to a halt at the little white-sheet tent. "May I have an orange and a cup of hot chocolate?" he said loudly.

The woman in the tent was sitting nodding. She jumped. "Gracious, boy, you scared me. You're the first customer in an hour. It isn't going good today. People either don't trust the ice, or they're waiting for Sunday."

"Do they skate on Sunday here?" Moonta asked in jealous amazement. "I wish we did."

"Where are you from?"

"Seven Houses," Moonta lied.

"Oh," the woman said, "but then aren't you too far from home with your little chair?"

"Oh, I don't really need the chair," he boasted. "I've got a stiff knee, so it's better to rest my weight on the back of the chair. I've got to go to the New Church's Pipe, and I thought it'd go better this way. . . . " At last he asked the big question, "Is it far?"

"It's a right stiff skate to the Pipe," the woman answered. "But being no skater, I've never been there by canal, so it's hard to tell. From here on the canal twists and turns so, I'd almost think it was five times farther than by road. But of course skates are ten times faster than feet—and you, you can always sit down on your chair when you're tired." She

197

scraped up Moonta's pennies from her orange crate counter.

Moonta stuck the orange in his pocket and gulped the hot chocolate. It wasn't hot; it wasn't even lukewarm. It was cold and a little nasty and gaggy. "I'd better hurry," he mumbled and took off behind his chair.

"Watch out for water holes," the woman called after him. "They tell me there's plenty, and in this poor county they don't bother to rope them off. Well, thank you, and now I may as well pull down my tent. With the thaw coming people get scared. Keep a weather eye out for holes, huh?"

The canal began winding just as the woman had said. Around the first bend, Moonta stopped. He hovered, waited, hoping the woman would do as she'd said and take down her tent and go home. After his boasting about going to the Pipe, it'd make him look pretty foolish to turn around now and go back past her tent. But the woman sat down again, made no motion to strike her tent. With a woeful sigh he turned to go up the canal. Suddenly he gave the chair a vicious shove ahead so he had to chase it. When he caught the chair again he was going full speed and kept going. Anyway, it was just as bad now to give up as to go on.

The canal started to wind more and more. Sometimes it almost made a complete turn, and then Moonta was facing the west. The dark cloud bank hanging there was hiding the sun. On the next half circle when he once more faced the west, he saw the rim of the sun sinking away below the cloud bank. The clouds weren't hiding the sun; the sun was going down.

The huge spreading cloud bank was reaching higher into the sky at the same time it was lowering over the land. The canal darkened. In the threatening dark a farmhouse rose up on one bank of the canal. Dogs barked, and one leaped down the bank and took out after him. But the dog skittered on the snowy ice, and gave up. He leaped back to the top of the safe bank, stood there sending his hoarse growling barks out after Moonta. Little shivers of after-scare ran up and down Moonta's back as he madly skated on.

If only there were people here. The canal lay so deep and lonesome. The darkness lay behind Moonta over the whole canal, almost as if, like the dog, it were chasing him. In flat fields smoke from chimneys was gray-white against the dark sky. Lights began to blink on in windows. That made it seem later and lonelier still.

Moonta's knee began to hurt steadily now. The tight bands that he had felt closing around his ankles screwed tighter still. Then it no longer was tightness; it was pain. Moonta winced with the pain, but he still wasn't sure. Maybe it was with his ankles as it had been with his knee—it only hurt when he was lonely and scared and wanted to go back. He told himself he was making it much worse than it really was—just to give himself an excuse to turn back.

He'd have to skate just as hard going back as he was skating

to go up the canal. His ankles would hurt just as much. Maybe it wasn't make-believe, though. He was so tired he was getting cold. He'd better slow down.

As Moonta slowly skated into the next bend he came to a narrow path in the snow. The path hadn't been made by a sweeper—it was too narrow, and there was snow on it still. It looked as if a sack or something had been dragged over the ice. He peered hard at it as he followed the path. He forced a curiosity that he didn't really feel just to keep himself going. Suddenly Moonta stopped and sat down on his chair in the little dragged path. He stooped over and rubbed both his ankles. Oh, it felt good—oh, they hurt. Oh, he was tired—oh, it felt good to sit down.

At a slight scraping sound Moonta jerked up. A big woman came bearing down on him straight down the narrow path. Now he knew what had made the dragged path in the snow. It was the woman's long skirts and coat. They swept over the snow on behind her. She skated clumsily, with short, hesitant strokes, but she kept herself very straight. When she saw Moonta she started to turn, then she skated right up to him. "With a beginner with a chair," she said, grinning, "I needn't be ashamed."

"Ashamed?" Moonta asked.

"Yes, ashamed. You see, my ankles won't carry me, but I'm crazy about skating, so I come here whenever there's ice. This is the loneliest stretch on the whole canal; all that seems to come by here is an occasional distance skater. When they come whipping along, I just stand still until they're out of sight. You see, with my ankles I'm skating more on the sides of my shoes than my skates. I can't do it long, and I don't dare do it before other people, but at least I have fun. I made me a special coat and skating skirts for myself. See . . . now no one can see my feet."

She turned and skated away to show Moonta. Her heavy coat hung straight, her many skirts swept from under it. She turned and came back.

"You're funny," Moonta said. "You're just like my Aunt Cora. She's always poking fun at herself too." He swallowed in time. He'd almost said, "And she's big and fat too."

"Funny, huh?" the big woman said good-naturedly. "But you're tired, aren't you? Ankles hurt? Well, that comes to all beginners. Of course I have it all the time." She kneeled heavily, and began to rub his ankles. "You won't tell on me?" She laughed up at him. "My village would be shocked. I'm from the next village and I'm the minister's wife. But who are you, and where are you from?"

"From Weirom," Moonta told her, because he liked her. Why, she was just like Aunt Cora, and it was good to have somebody to talk to after being so long alone in the strangeness. "How far is it yet to the New Church's Pipe?" he asked her.

"The New Church's Pipe?" she said amazed. "You, a beginner, and daring that all the way from Weirom?"

"Oh, I've got to meet my father there," Moonta invented hastily.

"Well, let me see . . . the Pipe comes after about the third bend from here, when you round that you ought to see the Pipe."

"The third bend," Moonta said gratefully. "Oh, do you know what? I'm going to tell my Aunt Cora about you. All her life she's wanted to skate, and if I tell her how you do it, and if I teach her . . ."

"Tell her to come out here, and we two cripples will skate and have fun."

"Why don't you get yourself a chair?" Moonta demanded. "That's how I learned. Then most of your weight is on the chair instead of on your ankles, and you learn to skate right."

The big woman looked doubtfully at the little chair. "I see it's cracked already."

"Try me," Moonta begged. "I'll stand straight and use my skates as runners, and then I'll be just like a chair and you can push me ahead by my shoulders."

The woman patted him on the cheek. "You're a nice boy, but it's no use anymore. My ankles are turned for good. And you've still got to get to the Pipe. You get going."

Moonta was reluctant to leave her. He didn't feel cold and tired anymore; he felt easy. His ankles were stiff, but they didn't pain. . . . At a loss for what to do, he poked his hands in his pockets and felt the orange. He was suddenly hungry in his relief, but he couldn't stand there eating an orange before the nice woman. He ripped off his mitten, dug his thumb through the skin of the orange, and offered her half. He was half delighted, half dismayed that she took it. "Thank you. I brought nothing along in my hurry, and even a poor skater gets the ice-hunger."

That made Moonta remember the sandwiches. He tugged them out of his jacket pocket. They were a bit squashed, but he held one out to the minister's wife. "Aunt Cora made them for me."

Then he giggled aloud, for just like Aunt Cora, the minister's wife reached out for the sandwich, then pulled her hand back. "There's too much of me now for my poor ankles," she said. "When you're as big as I am you really ought to have four ankles. But you get going now. You can eat while you skate."

The New Church's Pipe wasn't around the third bend. There was nothing—nothing. Maybe because the canal banks were so high it seemed much darker here, dark and deathly still, except for a dog in the distance. Moonta felt terribly let down. Why had the nice woman lied to him—and she a minister's wife? No, she wouldn't lie. She must have thought it was only three bends in the canal. Maybe she didn't know. Maybe she just wanted to encourage him—the way Lees always did.

Moonta stood irresolute. The cloud bank that had been in the west was almost over him now. It lay over the canal, low, lowering, threatening. It looked as if the clouds were full of snow. They were certainly full of darkness.

It seemed almost better to go on than to turn back and face the lowering darkness. Time went so fast when you skated . . . maybe night was coming. Moonta reckoned miserably in his mind, but couldn't think what hour the moon had come out last night. What was the use; with a sky full of clouds the moon wouldn't shine anyway.

Maybe, he at last admitted to himself, he'd have to walk all the way back by road. He certainly couldn't skate in the dark with all the water holes in the ice. On the roads the dogs that guarded every farmhouse would bark and rush him. It would be awful. It would be the middle of the night before he got home—if he could find his way home by way of the roads.

All at once he was so overwhelmed and helpless and full of black woe, he would have liked to throw himself down on the ice and lie there and bawl.

To his weak-kneed relief a swift skater came racing toward him around the bend just ahead. For a moment it looked like Father—Father could come back this way from his Eleven-Towns Tour. In his hope and relief Moonta wasn't even scared. He made himself believe that Grandpa was walking back but that Father had risked coming back by the canals. Then he saw it wasn't his father at all. It had looked like it because this man was a speed skater too. Moonta stood hunched and still.

The speeding man would have raced right by him, but Moonta yelled after him: "Where is the New Church's Pipe?" It really sounded more like bawling than yelling but the man swished around with effortless ease and came swooping back. "What'd you say, son?"

"I can't find the Pipe. She said it was around the third bend, but this is the third bend, and there's nothing."

"Oh"—the man laughed—"you're a stranger here, eh? You

206

took the wrong turn. There's two canals meet here—one empties into the other; and if you don't know it, it's hard to tell which is which. Well, I'm going that way. Suppose you lay on?"

"But I've got this chair."

"Look," the man said, "we can't stand here. See that sky?"

"Is it going to snow?" Moonta asked anxiously.

"Snow, kid . . . it's going to rain. Its raining out there now. See those straight streaks down from the clouds? That's rain. It's going to be here in another ten, fifteen minutes. Well, I want to be home by then, and you should be at the Pipe."

The man grabbed the chair, held it behind him. "Just hang on to the bottom rung, and if you can't skate fast enough and your feet feel as if they're leaving the ice, just set your skates still and get a free ride. Here we go, because with rain water on top of rotten ice, all of a sudden you've got no ice; you've got a wet hide."

They went flying. Moonta tried his very best, but his feet simply wouldn't move in and out fast enough. The man hadn't been boasting. At times Moonta's feet literally left the ice, his skimming skates only touched it here and there. "Don't try, kid, just glide," the man yelled.

They swooped up the other canal. Now, coming back, Moonta could see where he'd made his mistake. The new canal went much straighter. But then suddenly the black of two water holes loomed up before them. There was nothing but an ice bridge between the two holes. He saw it from around the man's madly pistoning legs and got scared. The man noticed at once. "Don't hold back. Don't drag. If you get scared you go in the water. Speed is what does it. Now you skate too, with all your might. We'll make it."

Never had Moonta skated so hard. His heart was high in his throat, his breath came rasping. At the last moment as they swooped between the two water holes he closed his eyes.

The next moment the man swirled around and swirled Moonta with him. He laughed triumphantly. "See, what did I tell you? Speed does it every time. Ice has a toughness, and if you don't give it time to think, it doesn't sink."

Moonta looked back and shuddered. The narrow ice bridge between the two holes now looped down, the two ends were like the ends of a hammock. The water rushed in where the ice had gone down. The two water holes were making themselves one.

"Golly," the man said, "that sure was a paper ceiling. But we made it, and that's what counts. . . . Say, how long have you been skating?"

"Just today," Moonta gasped out.

"No! Say, you, boy, have got skating sense. When you got scared enough going over that thin ice, you were matching my strokes perfectly, stroke for stroke. And I don't want to sound out about it, but I'm champion of this county."

"Just today," Moonta said proudly again. But there was no

time to think about it. They raced on. Moonta let the man pull him. He had to get his breath back. After they'd skated around three or four bends there was a house on the bank. The man dug in his heels and ground to a stop. "I live here. My name is Sjoerd Sjoerdsma. So remember this house. And say about three or four years from now, come and find me, and we'll race. You're going to be a speed skater if I ever saw one. So remember, about three years from now. I won't be champion then anymore. You'll be three years older, but so will I, and some young fool will come along and beat me. But we'll race then, and if you beat me, I'll never speak to you again." He laughed. "And now get going, kid, because around this next bend is the Pipe. Get off this side of the bridge because under it is nothing but water. And if it starts to rain, get off and stay off. Go home by road. And, see you in three, four years."

Imagine, imagine, he'd been skating with a champion, a speed skater, a champion of this whole county. Father and Mother were only champions of their little village. Imagine! Moonta glowed. He kept looking back as he skated on. The man was still stooped at the canal steps of his house, undoing his skates.

Around the next bend was a bridge. It was a different bridge than Moonta had ever seen. Not straight up and square like all other bridges, it was more like a tunnel of brickwork. The enormous round hole yawned up at him, black and dark.

He skated toward it another few strokes, then he stopped. As he stood there it started to rain. Rain pelted down on the ice with a harsh, clattering sound. In moments the snow on the ice was full of round black rain holes. Now the rain was not dotting the snow anymore; it came lashing. Moonta stood bowed over the back of the chair staring into the tunnel. It was so dark that in spite of the rain it seemed almost light beyond the other end. It was all water inside the tunnel, just as the champion, Sjoerd Sjoerdsma, had said.

Then as Moonta still peered, two figures, skating tightly together, came in a wide swing around a bend beyond the bridge, came bearing down hard in the rain toward the black tunnel. Was it? It was, it was! That was Father, and behind him Grandpa. It was all water, rippling black water, under the bridge. Didn't they see it? Couldn't they see the black water?

"Stop, Father, stop!" Moonta screamed. He shut his eyes as if to help him tear his mouth open wider and scream still louder: "Father, stop! It's water, all water. Stop, stop, stop."

210

13

The Paper Ceiling

IT MUST be that Father and Grandpa couldn't see him through the black tunnel of the bridge. They didn't hear him in the hard rain. "Stop!" Moonta screamed one desperate time more. "Stop, Dad!"

Maybe his father suddenly heard him, or saw the dark water under the bridge; he dug in the heels of his skates so hard it swung him around. Grandfather couldn't stop that fast. He lost his hold on Father's hand as he whiplashed around. He came flying. He threw himself wildly about to stop his headlong rush toward the open water. He dug in the

211

heels of his skates, but he still came on, stumbling, stuttering, falling. Then he fell so hard the ice at the edge of the water hole broke under him. He went down.

Not knowing what he did, Moonta clutched his red chair to his chest, and, skates on his feet, flew up the worn path in the canal bank next to the bridge. He found the same kind of steep, slanting path leading down the bank at the other side of the bridge. He dug the heels of his skates into the mud of the guttering hollow path, and half fell, half plunged, down to the canal. The rain pelted cruel and hard.

Father was lying flat on the ice, edging himself toward the water hole. Grandpa was floundering and gasping and blowing, trying to keep his head pushed up above the water. The black, icy water was up to his chin. Grandpa tried to plow and stumble toward the ice edge of the water hole.

"Can you stand, can you stand?" Father was yelling.

"Yes, I'm standing," Grandpa said between his teeth. "But I'm sinking in mud up to my knees."

"Stand still," Father ordered. "Don't thrash about, don't move."

Then Moonta was there above his father. Father turned his face up. "You here?" He didn't finish. He saw the red chair. He grabbed it. He got up on one knee, broke the split chair over his knee, hooked the two halves together, ripped off his belt, and lashed it around the two pieces of chair. He thrust the length of chair at Moonta. "Get down. You're

212

lighter, you reach it out to Grandpa. I'll slide over the ice behind you and push you ahead. Hang on to that chair and never let go—even if you go in the water. Don't be scared. I'll have a good hold on your ankles. But I'll push you right to the edge of the hole."

Father all but flung Moonta and the chair to the ice. He shoved him ahead. He kept a fierce grip on Moonta's sore ankles. Moonta slid flat in the water over the wet ice. "Never let go," Father kept saying between set teeth, "not even if the ice feels as if it's giving way under you."

Moonta stretched out his arm; he poked the sloppy, bending chair sections out over the water hole. Still Grandpa couldn't reach it. Now Moonta's head was sliding over the hole, he was staring glary-eyed down into the black water right under his nose. Suddenly Grandpa grabbed the edge of the chair. Behind Moonta, Father began pulling, began crawling back. With that pull, Grandpa managed to suck his leg out of the mud and take a big step toward Moonta and the water's edge.

Between them they were almost pulling Moonta in two. Suddenly his knee cracked. It was strange that in such an awful moment you'd notice it. Even Father heard. "What was that? Not the chair?"

"No, my knee," Moonta gasped. Strangely, his knee almost immediately felt better. Slow step by slow step Grandpa came toward the ice as Moonta and the chair were pulled back by Father.

213

"It's better, getting better," Grandpa gritted. "I'm coming up. It's shallower now." With his chest Grandfather broke the ice. When it wouldn't break he pounded the ice edge with one fist. Big pieces broke away, the ice cracked under Moonta ominously, but step by slow step Grandpa moved toward the bank as he broke the ice. Now Father had crawled up the bank. He sat hunched and ready at the bottom of the deep, foot-dug path. "Now, Moonta, up and out of the way."

He crawled up the rain-slippery bank past Father. When he turned, Grandpa had flung the lashed-together chair back of him—it floated in the water hole. With skate heels dug in, Father stooped, grabbed Grandpa under the arms, and tugged him up out of the water. He staggered backward up the sloped path.

At last Grandpa crept up the path. He stayed there a long moment on hands and knees, very still. They were all so still that even above the rain sounds they could hear the water rattling out of Grandfather's coat, back into the water hole.

"That sounds too awful," Grandpa said. He crawled a few feet up the bank, then rested again on all fours, getting his breath back. It rasped through his chattering teeth. "That's the coldest bath I've had in years," Grandpa chattered. "And I didn't even need it."

"Never mind the thankful jokes now," Father said to him.

214

"Get that coat off, and let's wring it out. It'll be best to hang it on you again—keep the wind out. There's nothing colder than wind on wet clothes over a wet hide."

"Nonsense," Grandpa said. "You two are just as wet as I am—even though you just soaked it up, while I did it the honest, straightforward way."

Father simply pulled off Moonta's scarf and woolen cap, and put them on Grandpa. "He's young, but you with your rheumatism."

Between them, each grabbing an end, Grandpa and Father wrung out the thick overcoat until it creaked and looked all corkscrewed.

"Now let's get home fast," Father said. "If your dunking didn't make you too scared, let's still try it on ice. If we don't, we'll get home so late the women will worry themselves sick, and you'll catch your death of pneumonia."

"Sure, the canal," Grandfather said. "Who's scared? I don't have to be, I can't get any wetter. But the question now is how do we get out, if we all land in a water hole together?" He made a little shivering joke. "Go in that water hole, Moonta, and get that chair. We might need it for further rescue operations."

"No, but I need my belt," Father said. "I've had no practice at all skating with my pants down."

"I'll skate tight behind you and hold them up." Grandpa laughed.

216

"No. Moonta, your belt—you're not going to need it, you're not going to be skating."

Moonta whipped off his belt, and Father immediately tried it for size. "My gosh, you're big. It fits." Somehow that brought Father to his senses. "Hey, what are you doing here? Where's your mother?"

"Home," Moonta said. He had to face it now. "I sneaked away from the village. Dad, I just had to see the New Church's Pipe. . . . Guess now I won't get to see it, anyway."

"Huh?" Grandpa said. "You sure found it. So did I. Head first."

It was Moonta's turn to say, "Huh?"

"Sure," Father said. "What did you think it was? This bridge is the New Church's Pipe. I guess they call it a pipe, well, because the round brick tunnel under it looks like a giant pipe."

Moonta said nothing. He stared through the rain at the black tunnel and the pieces of chair bobbing in it. Only a bridge. Well, he'd never tell anybody how he'd imagined it rising black and straight and tall in the moonlight like a tower, like a monument even. He wasn't going to tell anyone —ever.

"Well, here's one man that's mighty glad you and your chair found it," Grandpa said.

"It was God's providence," Father said seriously. "Just the same," he promised grimly, "I'll take care of Moonta and

217

really warm his 'providence' once we get home. Your mother must be worried crazy. You gone, darkness, rain on the ice . . . Gosh, kid!"

"She was worried sick about you and Grandpa all day," Moonta pointed out in a small voice.

"Yes," Grandpa said. "Council of war. What do we do? If we walk home the rest of the way the women will have to worry till after midnight. But skating in the rain and the dark over this kind of ice . . . "

"It's a sweeping shower," Father pointed out. "There's light under the cloud bank, and most of it is over us now. And the moon might still come out. Do we risk it—I up ahead, Moonta on my shoulders as a lookout? He's got good young eyes. Then if the ice should give out, you've still got a chance to stop, and I might make it with a burst of speed."

"Oh, golly," Moonta broke in. "Just beyond where the canals meet, the ice is all gone. The man was a speed skater, and he took me on behind him between two water holes. But when we got over, the ice sank away, and then there was one big hole clear across the canal."

"I can't stand here any longer," Grandpa said. His voice shook, his whole body shook.

"Council of war over," Father said. "Skates off, and we trot along the canal past Moonta's hole. That'll warm and limber us up. But from there, we'll try to make it on the ice."

"My old eyes aren't too good," Grandfather said doubtfully.

"No, but with Moonta on my shoulder, we'll be about the same weight as you. Then if we make it, you can. Any distance we can make on skates will get us home that much sooner."

It started to rain harder. "Rain," Grandpa said. "I was an old fool to get us into this. But this morning how could I expect we'd get seven kinds of weather?"

Stiff and sore as Moonta was, it felt good to jog along the top of the canal bank—safe. Below in the rain the canal looked dreary and dangerous. The rain had washed all the snow into dirty, small ridges.

At last they came to the spot beyond the juncture of the two canals, where Moonta and Sjoerd Sjoerdsma had gone over the bridge of ice. It was gone now. Rain bubbled noisily in the big, open water hole that stretched off into the dark.

Then, coming around the next bend, Moonta looked over his shoulder and shouted, "The moon—the moon! It's coming out. It's going to be light."

"About the friendliest sight in the world," Grandpa said.

Father wasted no time admiring the moon. He ran thumb and finger along the runners of his skates and stripped the wet mud away. He lowered himself to the bank, lifted Moonta down, helped Grandfather. "Get all the mud and goo off so we don't break our necks," he ordered. "Then get those skates on as fast as possible. A little moonlight and less rain, and

219

we'll make it yet. But the moon won't last long; there are too many clouds."

The moment Father had his skates on he hoisted Moonta to his shoulders. "Put your legs around my neck. You're the lookout. Keep your eyes straight ahead for anything—snow ridges, water holes, cracks . . . !" Then he told Grandpa, "Father, you keep about thirty feet back. Keep saying things so we'll know you're behind us."

Father skated out into the canal with Moonta.

"Keep an eye on your grandpa—look back once in a while," he said softly. "He may need all his breath for skating and forget to call out to us. But watch that ice like a hawk."

Father was gaining speed while he talked. Moonta swayed on his shoulders. He clasped his hands around Father's forehead. Father wasn't skating sedately now with hands folded on his back. He was speed skating. He leaned forward, he swung his arms, he all but windmilled them. They were still gaining speed. The wetness of rain and wind slashed along Moonta's cheeks. He had to duck low to keep his eyes wide open, watch the ice, and still not overbalance his father.

"How's the old man doing?"

"He's skating like he always does—the old man's way," Moonta answered. "Long strokes and hands on his back."

"I can't waste my breath yelling," Father said. "Tell him to skate like me—use his hands and arms and all of him."

It seemed strange to order Grandpa, but Moonta shouted

back what Father had said. Grandfather tried, but he stumbled.

"He can't make his strokes short to match yours," Moonta told Father.

"If he could only catch the rhythm—skate smooth and fast . . . But I can't stop to show him," Father muttered. "We can't stand a moment on this watery ice. Hey, can't you sing something? Something fast and snappy."

Up on Father's shoulders Moonta's mind raced through all the songs he knew. "All I can think of is songs from the Psalter in church," he told Father.

"Fine for sitting in church, but so slow he'd soon be standing still," Father said.

It felt so safe with Father, Moonta couldn't help giggling, for he had a sudden picture—the three of them standing in the middle of a water hole, sinking away, singing psalms. But even while giggling he searched his mind. Then he chanted out: "A pickerel, a pickerel . . . "

"Hey, none of that! Father said. "This ice is paper-thin enough without you singing it worse."

"But I can't think of a thing."

"How about that old round, 'The Tower Clock of Harlem'? But make it fast. Crack the bell and crack the tower—we don't care if it falls, just so it lands behind us."

Moonta tried it out. "Faster," Father said. "Watch the flash of my skates in and out, and time your song to that."

Moonta sang fast. His tongue barely touched the words:

> *The tower clock of Harlem,*
> *It rings out thus,*
> *It rings out thus,*
> *With a bom-bam,*
> *And a bom-bam,*
> *And a booma-booma bam, bam.*

That was all there was to the song. Moonta had to sing it over and over.

From behind, Grandpa shouted out, "Keep it up, boy. Keep it up. My tired old legs seem to hear it, and they're responding like a couple of fire horses going out to a fire. Man, the way I'm windmilling now, if you could only hook me up, I could grind a sack of meal before we get home."

"The rain's stopping," Moonta yelled to Grandpa. "But the moon's going down in a cloud bank. It's getting dark."

"Never mind the weather reports," Father muttered breathlessly. "Sing. Don't stop for anything. Pull on my right or left ear, whichever direction you want me to swerve around water holes, but don't stop singing. We're past Seven Houses, aren't we?"

There was a water hole. Moonta tugged at Father's left ear, but to Grandpa he chanted:

The tower clock of Harlem,
And Grandpa, and Grandpa,
We're past Seven Houses—
Except there are nine.
And now there's a light.
It looks like a lantern,
Coming right up the middle of the canal.

"That worries me," Father said. "If that's your mother, she's desperate, doing that alone. Yell out to her. No, sing. Singing travels."

"What if it isn't Mother?"

"Sing!" Father said. "Who else would it be?"

Then Moonta hurriedly sang out:

The tower clock, Mother.
It rings out thus,
It rings out thus:
It's Moonta, it's Moonta.
It's Father and Grandpa.
It's all of us, and all of us.

He started the so-called song again, but his voice broke.

224

Mother was still far away—if it was Mother—for all he could see was a pinpoint of swaying light. Moonta tried once more, but all he could do was make a croaking sound.

"It's Moonta and all of us—we're safe," Father yelled out hoarsely.

A scream came back, thin, high, and anxious. "Moonta, is that you?"

Moonta screwed his eyes shut, opened his mouth to its widest, and screamed: "MOONTA!"

Now the distant lantern light came on at a terrible speed. Father speeded toward the coming light. At last Mother swept up to them. She didn't stop, she swung out ahead of Father. "I'll lead, we can't stand still. Are you all right? We can't skate far anymore. I ran up along the canal till the ice looked safe, then skated. If you're scared enough, you dare anything. . . . Follow me the moment I swerve to the bank."

Mother skated ahead so fiercely Father couldn't follow her swiftness with Moonta on his shoulders. From way back Grandpa called out: "Hey, wait for baby. I want coffee, too."

In just a few more moments Mother swooped toward some dug-out steps in the canal bank. One by one they followed her, ripped off their skates, and climbed stiffly up the steps.

Mother sat down on the muddy, wet top step. "Just go on by," she whispered. "Don't say anything. Give me a moment."

"Are you up to it now?" Father asked at last.

Mother looked at him. "Up to what?" she said.

"The whaling I'm going to give Moonta right here and now, for the way he disobeyed and worried you."

"Hold it," Grandpa said. "I thought of it first—early this morning."

Mother got up. "Maybe we should all take turns," she said wearily.

"Oh, no you don't," Moonta said hastily. "You're all too late. The sweeper has it all done. Maybe I've got this one coming, but I didn't have that one coming—and he really whaled the stuffing out of me." He had to tell them all about

226

it, and as he'd expected, Father and Grandfather roared.

"Do you think it's enough for the way you've been behaving?" Mother asked. "I don't know what's got into you."

"Yes, it's enough, Mother," Moonta said. "I don't know either. I guess it was everything at once. But now I can skate, and it's different."

"Then get your land legs under you and run. Aunt Cora is searching the water holes along the canal. And I know the hells she's going through. Run!"

Moonta ran long, before he saw Aunt Cora's lantern light. Aunt Cora was going along the canal bank, holding the lantern down on a rope to light the water holes. Now she was on her knees, peering down the bank. "Aunt Cora," he yelled.

She jumped as if she'd been shot. Her hand went to her heart; she actually panted. "Moonta, no! And safe on the road. I thought I saw a stocking cap your color in this water hole— my lantern's gone sooty. But it was just an old rag in the canal, and there you are on the road."

She dropped her lantern, she grabbed him, she squashed him against her. "I ought to skin you alive—I ought to. But run, because the headmaster is across the canal somewhere, thinking to fish you out of every water hole. . . . And I oughtn't to tell you, but Lees says there's going to be ice again on Monday."

"Ice?" Moonta said, astounded. "No!"

"She says the moon's going to chase all the changeableness

away, and it's going to freeze hard again, starting in the morning."

"Oh, golly, Aunt Cora," Moonta shouted, "then Monday I can teach you. Oh, skating is wonderful!" Hurriedly he told her about the minister's wife. "All you need is long skirts and a long, heavy coat—it hides your ankles and your skates and everything. She wants you to come skate with her, and Monday I'm going to teach you. You wouldn't want to learn with a chair, but you can use me. I'll be just like a sleigh on runners, and you can push me by my shoulders. Aunt Cora, I can do it—why, I skated with Sjoerd Sjoerdsma, and he's the county champion. . . . Oh, you've got to learn."

"Imagine," Aunt Cora said, "you thinking of me. But run— there's the headmaster's lantern now; he's come back around this side of the canal. Run—show him you're alive."

Moonta hesitated. "If I had a sheet, maybe he'd think I was a ghost," he joked nervously, and didn't budge.

"Will you go?" Aunt Cora said fiercely. "He's been worried sick about you. And the pea soup and sausage are waiting, and will get colder than the canal."

Still Moonta hesitated, hating to face the headmaster. Now they could hear Mother, Father, and Grandpa coming down the road. Moonta waited, hoping that if they came up before the headmaster reached him and Aunt Cora, everything would get forgotten in talk.

"Are you going?" Aunt Cora said. "What do you think?

He's been blaming himself all afternoon for being too severe with you, sending you off the canal. And then you had to go and do this desperate, willful thing—going way out the canal."

"He doesn't have it in for me?" Moonta asked, unwilling. Aunt Cora gave him a shove.

Moonta jogged slowly toward the coming lantern light, holding his pants up with both his hands. He stopped in the safe dark, well before he reached the headmaster. "Master, it is I," he called out carefully. "Moonta. And Grandpa and Father are coming with Mother, and everything is all right."

"Thank God, thank God," the headmaster said. He came fast.

It was hard to say, but Moonta hastily said it: "Master, I'm sorry."

"So am I," the headmaster said. He stopped before Moonta and held the lantern high as if he had to make sure. "I'm sorry about us both. You may not have realized it, but things could have got ugly there at *The Six Brothers.* You know our villagers—they were ready to tear things apart. But I was angry, too. We both acted in anger, and we both are big enough to have more sense than that."

When the headmaster saw Moonta's scared face in the raised lantern light, he suddenly laughed. "I guess I wasn't any better peacemaker than you. Maybe I ought to charge myself five hundred of your thousand peacemaker lines.

Five hundred for me, five hundred for you—come Monday."

"Oh, but Lees says there's going to be ice on Monday," Moonta said. It was all he could think to say.

"Lees said ice? Well, then there'll be ice."

To Moonta's amazement the headmaster wasn't laughing or joking. He believed about Lees, the way all the kids did!

"So Lees said ice. And here come your folks and Aunt Cora. We'd better strike a quick bargain—I'll tell you what. I'll cancel your five hundred lines, you cancel mine, and we'll both skate on Monday. Come on, let's go meet them."

Together Moonta and the headmaster hurried up to the four dark marching figures in the road. Mother had doused her lantern. Aunt Cora's still smoked on. Suddenly Moonta had to shout out at them. "Mother," he yelled, "Father, Grandpa—Lees says there's going to be ice Monday. And . . . and we're going to have pea soup for supper."

"Pea soup," Grandpa said hungrily. "For that I'll go into the canal any day."

"Pea soup with sausage!"

"For that—twice a day."

"Yes, but Mother, Father . . . Oh, Master, I forgot—but I'm going to race with Sjoerd Sjoerdsma!"

"Sjoerd Sjoerdsma, the champion?" Father said, amazed.

"Sure. He wants me to race in about three years. Now I know I can really skate."

"Will that change everything?" Mother asked softly. "Tomorrow in church do I pray for a thaw, or—as you asked me —do I pray the other way?"

"The other way, Mother," Moonta assured her gravely. "And Lees said it'll be ice, and I'm going to teach Aunt Cora, and I'm going to skate with Master Andries, and . . . and— Suddenly he thought of it, and almost crowed his delight. "Why, we almost skated like a family for a few moments back there a while ago. But Monday we can skate as a family—and I'll be in it too!" He let out his breath in a deep, amazed sigh.

"Yes, but did I hear mention of pea soup?" the headmaster said. "And am I invited?"

"Oh, would you come?" Mother said delightedly.

"Woman," the headmaster joked, "that'd be an unnecessary question even from a first grader. Would I come for pea soup and sausage!"

Moonta practically danced up to his mother. "Lees, too, Mother. Lees, too."

"Of course! Lees belongs."

"Then I'm going to run and tell her. Mother, Dad—everybody, I've got to run. I've just got to."

Almost together Grandpa and Father warned: "Watch those pants."

Moonta laughed, hoisted his britches, and holding them up with both hands, ran like the wind.

Format by Kohar Alexanian
Set in Linotype Caledonia
Composed by Wolf Composition Co., Inc.
Printed by The Murray Printing Company
Bound by The Haddon Craftsmen, Inc.
HARPER & ROW, PUBLISHERS, INCORPORATED